IN VACATIONLAND

New Fiction from the Real Maine

Edited by Mark Melnicove

1985

The Dog Ear Press
South Harpswell, Maine

Dedicated to Kendall Merriam,
who has been here since the beginning.

Library of Congress Cataloging in Publication Data
Main entry under title:

Inside vacationland.

    Contents: Crowe Bovey's burning-cold/by Carolyn Chute — The Maine food plan/by Sanford Phippen — The ice fish/by Willis Johnson — [etc.]
    1. Short stories, American — Maine.   2. Maine — Fiction.
I. Melnicove, Mark.
PS548.M2I67 1985   813'.01'0832741   85-7074
ISBN 0-937966-18-5 (pbk.)

Acknowledgments

"Crowe Bovey's Burning-Cold," ©1984 by Carolyn Chute, first appeared in *Agni Review 20*. Reprinted by permission of the author.

"The Ice Fish," ©1983 by Willis Johnson, is a revised version of a story which first appeared in *Yale Review*, Summer, 1983. Reprinted by permission of the *Yale Review* and the author.

"Squatter's Rights," ©1979 by Fred Bonnie, is the title story from *Squatter's Rights*, Oberon Press, Ottawa, 1979. Reprinted by permission of the author.

"Smoke," ©1977 by Lucy Honig, first appeared in *Dark Horse*, number 13. Reprinted by permission of the author.

The publication of "Claire's Song" by Kendall Merriam in this volume is made possible, in part, by a grant from the *Maine State Commission on the Arts and the Humanities*.

Special thanks to the following for their invaluable help in putting together this book: Sheila Garrett, Eleanor Young, Sandy Gregor, Mitch Goodman, Deborah Gould, Diane Moran, George Gibson, Sarah Robbins, Cynthia Jenson, Richard Wood, Bau Graves, Phyllis O'Neill, Cooder and Anya.

Printed in the United States of America.

First Edition

INSIDE VACATIONLAND
New Fiction from the Real Maine

CONTENTS

INTRODUCTION

No one seems to know the exact origin of the term the "real" Maine, but like it or not, it has become a part of our vocabulary. Even *Down East* magazine, whose articles and photographs are often pointed to as the epitome of what the "real" Maine *is not*, has begun to use the term.

Although it is impossible to define exactly the "real" Maine, there is a tradition of sweeping it under the rug, hiding it from view, and not talking about it, at least in print. For decades, Maine was "Vacationland", that idyllic paradise of rock-bound coasts, aged pine trees and local yokels. It's still seen that way by some; how else to explain this year's State Development Office advertising slogan which urges people to come to Maine, "the Great Escape". But for those who live here year-round and who can't escape, or who don't want to; for those who know another Maine, the slogan doesn't quite ring true.

Unfortunately, this selling of the state has permeated the atmosphere of too much Maine literature. Until recently, inside views of Maine people and their lives were published infrequently. And when they were, they usually did not get the attention they deserved. Fred Bonnie's two collections of short stories, both published in Canada and given virtually no circulation in Maine, are an excellent case in point.

The most outspoken proponent for a new realism in Maine literature has been Sanford Phippen. Since 1976, in his columns in *Maine Life* and *Puckerbrush Review,* and over MPBN Radio, he has complained that *his* Maine, "the Maine I know in my heart, soul and guts; the Maine I grew up in; the Maine I both love and hate; the Maine that is in my blood and ancestry and will haunt me always," was "missing" from the "great bulk of Maine's popular literature."

"The picture is way off-balance in favor of the Year-Round Summer People and the Maine Mythologists," he wrote in 1980, "who have combined forces along publisher's row to continue to hype the Maine that never was."

Eventually, Phippen got so worked up about this sad state of affairs that he wrote the Maine stories he wanted himself. The result was *The Police Know Everything*, first published in 1982, and now (early 1985) in its fifth printing.

The big breakthrough, however, has come with Carolyn Chute and her first novel, *The Beans of Egypt, Maine*, a national best-seller. It is heartening to see such a daring book get the wide readership it deserves and to sense that the door is now open for other fiction from the "real" Maine to be heard.

Chute's and Phippen's are but two perspectives. Obviously, there are as many "real" Maines as there are voices to portray them. *Inside Vacationland*, the first collection of its kind, is a celebration of that fact. In the pages that follow you will find a wonderful diversity of vision and experience from Willis Johnson's Russian community of "Plankton", to Rebecca Cummings' Finns of Oxford County; from Kendall Merriam's intimate view of a woman sardine factory worker, to Dan Domench's portrait of Maine hucksterism gone haywire.

But this is only a taste, the tip of the iceberg, so to speak. Besides the ten authors represented here, there are other Maine writers unsung, unpublished or known only through the small press, who have yet to be heard by a general audience. It is my hope that *Inside Vacationland*, by bringing together these stories, will encourage others to write, publish and read more about Maine.

Mark Melnicove

INSIDE VACATIONLAND
New Fiction from the Real Maine

CROWE BOVEY'S BURNING-COLD
Carolyn Chute

The Junkyard: Sunday, 7 a.m.

The scout crow, lean in winter, makes a sweep over the outer ring of wrecks and junks. Everything is sealed in new snow. The scout crow opens his toes and swings down to perch on the boom of the yard tractor. He checks for signs of life but finds only the now-and-then plop of snow from hoods and fenders.

Over the Drugstore: Same time.

The room is hot and the bedcovers are in a ball on the floor. The only thing Crowe Bovey is wearing is his metal-rimmed glasses. He pokes at Jill Luce. She's not really sleeping, just pretending... holding back a giggle. Jill's body breathes and unbraids, the stomach muscles careening porpoise-like. When Jill Luce is wearing clothes, they are the kind with high waists. Crowe Bovey pokes at her again and the waterbed rolls. Jill pretends to have a dream. Whimpers. Crowe Bovey listens to Jill's FM radio, hard rock, up on his elbows. He has a long broad body, but short legs. His hands are often darker than his body . . . tattooed by auto grease. His eyes slide contemptuously over the posters on the wall. On the closet door is the Van Halen lead in leather pants and heavy chains. The chained man's face is as unalarmed as a half-dozing baby. Crowe picks the label off the coffee jar on the nightstand and shreds it, shreds it some more. He opens his hand and the shreds flutter on Jill like colored snow. She opens her eyes. He locks himself to her for another round. They have not left this hot place for three days.

On Seavey Road: Same day, an hour and a half later.
Volunteers shout over the grind of pumps while water rumbles down the timbers that have caved into the cellar. You can't tell a child's wristbone from a pencil in the black debris and mud.

A neighbor just arriving sighs: "Lost them all, didn't they?"
Another neighbor nods.

"I seen a couple of them yesterday . . . in the window there. All girls, weren't they?"

"Yip . . . two redheads, three blondes."

A whisper: "They just found the mother . . . what's left, that is."

More neighbors arrive, parking beyond the firehoses. "I don't see Crowe's truck. Where's HE at?" a neighbor in bedroom slippers asks as she rocks from foot to foot, hugging herself.

Another neighbor shrugs.

The hoses kick. Water sprays on some of the neighbors. They shield their faces with their hands. "This will make the Portland papers," one neighbor says through his fingers.

"Maybe TV," says a young boy.

"Where's the father? Maybe he doesn't know yet."

"Ain't seen his truck for three days," says the bedroom slippers woman.

"THREE DAYS!"

A fellow in dress-up clothes moves among them with a TV camera on his shoulder. He aims it at some of the neighbors.

Between the dozens of cars and trucks and three rescue units along the road glides the new pickup truck of Crowe Bovey. The slush whispers.

"Jesus! There he is."

As he steers with one hand, he pulls at his cheek with the other, his habit. You can't see his eyes for the gray day, and black tree limbs scutter over his metal-rimmed glasses. His green work-shirt which reads *Letourneau's Used Auto Parts* on back is buttoned to the throat.

Rescuers move over the ice with his wife's mother between them. She has just arrived in her station wagon. Neighbors have become silent. The mother-in-law makes gagging cries and wrenches at the rescuers' orange jackets. The rescuers slide away from her and toward her like comic skaters.

Crowe Bovey shuts off his engine and gets out. His dark hair is streaked gold from working bareheaded. He stands with the neighbors among the firehoses and watches the volunteers flood the timbers, the timbers steaming and hissing like a dragon fighting back. He watches his mother-in-law go onto her knees, her red screaming face in folds like the dewy rose. Then he looks into some of the neighbors' faces. They avert their eyes.

After a minute he gets back into his rig, turns around on the slushy crown, then drives back up Seavey Road like he's just a curious neighbor going back home.

At the Junkyard Gate: Same day, just before dark.

Crowe Bovey parks his new pickup at the locked gate. He sits with the windows rolled up, his hand on the wheel. He watches a single crow circling over the wrecks and junks. The crow almost playfully dips as it passes over the junkyard office. Now Crowe Bovey sees the others on the woodline, a tree of crows waiting, more than he can count.

In the House Behind the Junkyard: Same time.

Jordan Letourneau's wife hangs shirts in the kitchen. The shirts are green and say *Letourneau's Used Auto Parts* on the backs in gold. On the pockets they say: *BOSS*. The kids walk the kitchen counters like cats.

In the House behind the Junkyard: Next day, 8 a.m.

Jordan Letourneau's wife Clair sleeps in a tangle of blankets alone. She loves to sleep. When she hears the first shot, she pulls a pillow over her head. The second shot. She sits up, blinking. She jumps up in her nightgown which is pinned at the neck with a safety pin and runs barefoot to the piazza. Her kids are already up, walking the kitchen counters. They run to the piazza with her and stare out into the brightness with round hazel eyes. A splatter of black feathers lies beneath a tree and out of this two skinny legs stick straight up. Another splatter of feathers lies a few yards away. Crowe Bovey stands coatless in the opening between lilacs, a shotgun across his thighs.

"What are you DOING!!!" Clair screams.

Crowe Bovey smiles.

Clair leans down and makes a loose snowball from snow on the step. She pitches it at his face, but he ducks, trotting away, laughing.

At the Funeral Parlor: Wednesday, 10 a.m.

He sits square-shouldered in his only clothes, his workshirt buttoned to the throat. It says *Letourneau's Used Auto Parts* on his back . . . *CROWE* on the pocket. Among the reds and whites and golds of flowers along the wall, members of the family embrace. The room is vaporous with their sobs. And the room is a little stinky from velvet curtains, Afghan rugs, and years and years of dark light.

Now and then one or two of them look over at the dark circle of chairs where Crowe Bovey sits, and search his face for signs of grief.

In the House Behind the Junkyard: After the funeral.

When big freckled Clair Letourneau comes to the door of her bedroom, she sees her husband's tranny man at the table, pulling his cheek and three days' whiskers. Clair rubs her eyes with her palms. "Gawd, it's YOU," she says. Snow whirls outside the windows and the lilac bushes only a few yards away are lost in the brilliance.

Still in their pajamas, Clair's children scurry over the kitchen counters. "GET OFF THEM COUNTERS!!!" she screams, and the children plop off all at once with a box of Lucky Charms.

When she sees the shotgun, she raises one eyebrow.

Crowe Bovey says: "Your husband SAID I could stay here a few days till I get situated. I been sleepin in my Ford." He wipes the shotgun with a soft cloth, his fingers pressing along the thickness of the barrel in hard elongated strokes.

Clair wonders why he isn't with Jill Luce . . . nineteen-year-old Jill Luce with the high hard-on-the-ears giggle and all those high hard shoes. Everybody in town knows about Jill Luce and Crowe Bovey. She wonders what has come between them. She yawns. Her lavender eyes water. "Well, well, well . . . here we are. Jordan, what a pig-ass . . . he don't tell me nuthin. You never know who's gonna turn up here . . . every mornin's a new surprise! Drunks on the floor . . . half-wits watchin my TV . . . I come out in my nightclothes and BINGO! . . . a new face!"

The kids arrange plastic bowls on the floor, shake cereal into them, then pour on milk. They eat without spoons like cats.

Crowe Bovey watches his boss's wife with a haughty half-smile.

"Why you got that gun in here around my kids?"

"Ain't loaded."

She sniffs. "Yep . . . my husband has what you call a HEART OF GOLD!"

He watches her hard. Her bleached hair lays sticky on her neck like a deflated yellow balloon. Her big freckles seem to churn.

The kids leave their bowls with milk and soggy cereal and get out their police cars, fire trucks, school buses, and wee sporty cars. One child tips a bowl and the milk runs down the slanted floor with colored cereal spinning on top.

"Quit FOOLIN AROUND!!" Clair screams. She fidgets with the safety pin on her gown. Crowe Bovey watches the fingers on the safety pin. His half-smile is eerie for his eyes are expressionless, fixed.

Clair exclaims: "Kids! This is the man Daddy sent up here to be with us for today! Maybe LONGER. He ain't as bad as the last one. You guys ain't forgot HARRY, have ya? Harry, that one day before yesterday."

They all shake their heads and scrinch up their noses.

The dark spotty light of the kitchen crawls over Crowe's glasses.

"THIS one's just a crow killer," says Clair.

One kid runs its tongue out at Crowe Bovey.

Crowe's eyes slide onto the children. He cracks his knuckles. With wet red smiles the kids all watch him do this. They copy him.

Clair pads barefoot to an open drawer and takes out a spoon. Crowe fondles his gun, the heavy almost black wood, but his eyes are on Clair's broad back.

None of the kids can get sound to come out of their knuckles. They pull on their fingers in various ways.

The tranny man leans back on two legs of the chair. "You . . . Clair," he says. "You pretty sentimental 'bout crows, huh?"

A stiffness seizes Clair's face.

The kids pull each others' fingers. At last a sharp CRACK! A scream. "Aw-wahhhh!"

Clair crosses the slanted floor to inspect the finger. "For crissakes! Would you guys find somethin to do! Ain't *Sesame* on?"

They rush for their toy cars.

Clair starts coffee.

The storm shakes the house, shrieks across the openness of the junkyard.

Clair watches the coffee beating up inside the glass knob.

The kids roll the cars and trucks down the steeply slanted floor. They shriek to imitate sirens. The trucks smash into the wall. "Not so ROUGH!!" Clair screams.

They do it again and again and again.

Clair watches the coffee beating darker, darker, darker.

Crowe Bovey pulls his cheek and the kids standing along the wall pull their cheeks.

Clair says: "You guys go see if *Sesame's* on."

They stretch their cheeks grotesquely. One cheek makes a snapping noise as it lets go.

Clair keeps her back to them all, listening to the storm rattle the house. She hears Crowe Bovey's wet boots shift under the table, but the kids are strangely quiet.

The tranny man's eyes on Clair's back are like the eyes of a soldier at attention.

Clair wishes she were back in bed. She pours two mugs of coffee. When she turns she sees all three kids on the table while the tranny man lets them feel the gun. "GET DOWN!!" she screams. They plop down like cats. As she runs at the table some of the hot coffee sloshes over her hands.

The kids vanish.

Crowe Bovey rocks slowly on the back legs of his chair. Standing near him she can smell his dirty shirt and dungarees, the blackened hands. He smells like the inside of a motor running hot.

Clair holds her burned hand hard against her gown.

He pulls a mug toward him.

"Don't you want milk?" she asks.

He shakes his head.

She straddles the chair across from his.

"He's payin me a dollar a crow, you know. Maybe you don't know that. He wants em cleaned up," he says, smiling.

"He?"

He almost giggles. "HIM! Your husband!"

Clair looks grief-stricken.

"You have a CROW PROBLEM HERE," Crowe says.

"They just FLY AROUND," she says.

He chuckles. "They do more than fly around. They are BAD NEWS!"

Clair leans forward, her eyes fluttering. "HE ain't here. He's gone. On a drunk. HE ain't got nuthin to say. You shoot any more crows and I'll call the deputy to lug you off, Mister Man."

He wipes his mouth on his sleeve. "You're dumb," he says softly. He swallows deeply of the coffee. Steam charges up around his glasses. "DUMB. Crows are useless. They have no purpose."

"I LIKE em," she says icily. She adds canned milk to her coffee . . . stirs it . . . the spoon clinks.

"I've been huntin crow since I was five years old. I musta blasted two thousand a them cocksuckas so far. POW!" He aims a pretend gun. The invisible gun kicks his shoulder.

Clair glares at him.

The tranny man leans back on the chair legs, rocks to and fro. "I ain't got a dot of mercy for them bastardly things," he says.

"You're a weird man," she says.

"Ain't nuthin wrong with killin. You like meat dontcha?"

She fiddles with her safety pin. He watches her pulling hard on the pin. "Maybe," she says.

"Maybe, maybe," he jeers. His lip curls.

"I think you looked pretty SILLY the other day pickin on them birds with your stupid ol . . . CROW GUN."

Crowe laughs a high ominous shriek. "Ain't any CROW GUNS. Boy! You know a lot!"

"Whatever."

"There's no gun called a crow gun, Clair."

"Don't matter."

He puts his head down and kisses the gun. "This dandy is a Marlon pump action twelve gauge. It's a SHOTGUN, see . . . a SHOTGUN."

"Big deal!"

"Well, if you wanna learn something instead of being dim."

The Junkyard: The next day.

Clair Letourneau's kids dress themsleves. They watch the junkyard men strip junks for the crusher. They run over the tops of cars like cats. They find Crowe Bovey pulling a transmission behind the office. He works his wrench fast so that short wizened breaths fly frozen from his face. His hands are wrecked with sores. In time the kids find the crows in the bed of Crowe Bovey's truck. The uncounted PILE of crows. They stand on the back bumper and look at each other with awe quivering in their round hazel eyes. "Yukk!" they say. They pat the dead crows.

In the House Behind the Junkyard:
Same day, almost midnight.

His glasses are next to the lamp. He sleeps on the divan without taking off his wet boots. The front room has taken on the scent of his dirty shirt and dungarees. He lies on his face.

Clair's children cross the old fern-print linoleum . . . munching. Their hands go in and out of cereal boxes. They stand at the edge of the divan and look down on Crowe Bovey, at the back of his shirt which says *Letourneau's Used Auto Parts*. They look at each other solemnly. One of them drops a handful of Apple Jacks on the shirt. They wait. The shirt rises and falls . . . uninterrupted. They look at each other. Another hand opens over the sunstreaked hair . . .

The Junkyard: The next day.

She wears a coat over her gown. She seldom dresses. As she steps off the piazza, huge pieces of frozen breath are tugged from her face by the subzero wind. She sees the tranny man has made a path in the snow with his comings and goings. His new pickup is parked on the edge of the junkyard close to the lilacs that obscure her old house. The openness of the junkyard is noisy with wind. She follows the tranny man's path swinging her arms. As she passes the truck, she hears him. "Twenty-eight, twenty-nine, thirty, thirty-one . . ."

"What are you DOING?" she says.

"Countin," he says.

She pulls up on the tailgate with both hands.

"A buck a crow, " he says grinning.

Only a small part of her freckled face shows inside her hood. Her eyes move over the crows . . . crow heads, crow feet, pieces of crows, whole crows, and on this pile Crowe Bovey is squatted, one hand on one knee . . . large grinnin mouth. Slowly she lowers herself back to the ground.

In the House Behind the Junkyard:
Several days later.

There is another storm. Clair emerges in her faded gown. He is at the table playing with a book of matches. Snow plops off his boots, drizzles away down the slanted floor. He doesn't look up. His smell is more enormous. There is a bloodiness on the table under his hands. And nearby is the two-week-old *Evening Express* with the headline: SIX KILLED IN MORNING BLAZE. There are fingerprints in blood and grease like dark feathers on the edges.

Clair takes egg salad from the refrigerator. "If you WANT some clean clothes, you can wear some of Jordan's," she says.

He cracks his knuckles. This time the kids don't copy. They just hang close to Clair. When Clair turns, she sees the man has shredded the matchbook cover and popped off all the match heads.

There's a buzz in the distance.

"Is that Jordan comin up to plow us out?" Clair asks.

Crowe puts his face close to the window. He nods.

"Oh boy," says Clair. She puts the egg salad and a loaf of cheap bread on the table. The round gray eyes of her children watch her hands make the sandwiches.

The buzz comes through the storm, closer, closer.

The kids watch the tranny man shred the envelope to the light bill.

Clair says: "You kids ain't gonna eat this dinna . . . you're probably all full up on cereal. Crowe makes shreds of the shreds, smaller and smaller shreds.

Clair passes out the sandwiches.

The plow clatters into the dooryard. The kids clutch their

sandwiches and run to the window. Clair sighs. "Well, kids . . . here's Daddy in his truck, home at last from his wine, women, and song! Bet he's hungover and ugly as a bear. Let's see what he wrecks THIS time. Last time he crumpled your swingset . . . remember?"

They all nod. Their mouths tear at the sandwiches.

Crowe breaks his sandwich into four equal pieces with his black gashed fingers . . . arranges them to cover the headline of the paper.

Jordan is plowing so close to the house now that the glasses and plates in the cupboard clang together. Clair says almost cheerfully: "Don't that man LOVE TO PLOW! He's a real artist with the snowplow . . . ain't he, kids?"

The kids chew slowly, staring wide-eyed into the crazy soaring lights. One child's cheeks are flushed violet. It stands off to one side, opening its sandwich and studying the egg salad.

Jordan backs up, rams the snow higher, higher, higher.

The flushed child rolls its shoulder against its mother's thigh, against the faded gown. "Poor sick baby," Clair sighs. She stoops to wipe its nose with the hem of her gown. The tranny man's eyes widen on the bare freckled leg.

"Baby's got the bug," says Clair.

The child's bleak round hazel eyes are like night eyes. Its hair is flat with sweat. Crowe Bovey moves his eyes up and down the feverish child. The child throws its sandwich on the floor. "STOP THAT!!!" Clair screams.

The spinning light on the truck cab fills the kitchen, drizzles over Crowe Bovey's glasses. Clair pulls out a chair, straddles it, and the feverish child straddles her. "What the hell's that under my foot!" She looks under the table. It's the egg sandwich.

The other kids get tired of watching the plow job. They vanish.

Suddenly the sound of the TV in the front room is louder than the plow. The channels switch crazily. Clair screams: "SHUT IT OFF!!"

But they don't.

Meanwhile the old rowboat in the yard splinters to a million pieces. Jordan backs up, rams it again.

The TV goes louder. Clair supposes one child is in front of the TV working the knobs, the other on top of it working the rabbit ears. She can't understand what makes her children so cat-like.

The plow rams the house and the plaster from the tall ceiling clatters across Crowe Bovey's dungarees. "Jesus!" he gasps.

Clair kisses her child's hot face. She looks across the table at the tranny man who is half-standing, striking the plaster from his legs.

Along the edge of the house Jordan Letourneau makes snow hang in vertical bluish walls high as the house. The monstrous snow. The amber light on the cab churns through the kitchen, gleams on the tranny man's glasses. Crowe flexes his fingers.

The child rolls its face between Clair's breasts.

Jordan rams snow to the east and west, his rear wheels spinning, whining. The snow heaves up, covers one back window.

"That's funny!" Clair chirps. "Crowe kills crow!" She laughs deeply and her broad shoulders quake.

The plow thumps around the yard, eats up the rubbish barrel. Snow explodes against the back door. The headlights flood the kitchen with hard steady light.

The child fills up its fingers with Clair's gown and one obscured nipple.

The tranny man goes white.

The hand of the child is like a gray spider moving with sureness.

Clair's lavender eyes tear up with laughter. "Crowe kills crow!" she shrieks.

The man stands with his bleeding black hands away from his body and the yellow light sweeping across his belt buckle, making it glimmer. "It ain't THAT funny." His voice is coarse.

The headlights of Jordan's truck pull away then burst in at a different side of the kitchen. Clair says: "What if one day a crow shoots you . . . crow shoots CROWE!!!" She makes a high witch-like cackle.

"You talk STUPID!" Crowe cries. "Them goddam cock-suckas are takin over! I read just last week that crows in the Northeast are breedin so fast that if we don't control em, we'll be swamped with crows. You can't be a bleedin heart about this for crissakes!"

He pushes his glasses up, rubs his eyes hard . . . blows his cheeks in and out. "That's what GOD puttem here for! For our pleasure!"

"PLEASURE!" Clair screeches.

"Yes! It says in the BIBLE that MAN SHALL HAVE DOMINION OVER ALL THE BEASTS. That's what it says!"

Clair rolls her eyes. "I KNOW what it says." She leans forward and hisses: "Dominion don't mean KILL." The child whimpers into Clair's ribcage.

Crowe steps over the cereal bowls, trucks, and tricycles and in the swirling lights flexes his back and shoulders. His shirt is partly tucked in, partly yanked out. "You ain't one of them Christly loonytoon environmentalists are ya?" he snorts.

"I don't know. What's one of them?"

He pushes his hands into his pockets.

The child sucks through the gown at the enlarged nipple. The child's eyes are on the tranny man, its cheeks red like a clown's.

"It's what all women are!" cries out the tranny man. He paces. He almost brays: "I love to hunt crow." His eyes are on the sucking mouth. "It's neat. When you're after em, you pit your intelligence against one of God's smartest birds!"

The child wrings the gown-covered nipple with its teeth. "Ah Sweetie," Clair murmurs. "You ain't gonna get nuthin THAT way."

The man's bottom lip trembles.

The child's mouth slips and the soft walls of it make a rude noise.

The man wheels around the room. The smell of his dirtiness toils toward Clair as he passes.

The plow strikes the house. The walls moan. Crowe cries: "What's he tryin ta DO!!! Kill us?"

"He always does this," Clair says softly.

He laughs, rubs his hair. "That ol boy means business, don't he?" He blows his cheeks in and out. He cracks his knuckles. Clair sees his mouth is wet at the corners.

He swings his arms, punches one palm with the other fist.

Clair rocks from side-to-side with the child. She blows across the red cheek. The more she fondles the child, the more excited the man gets. He watches her tracing the damp little head. He paces up and down the slanted floor, stepping over school buses and wee sporty cars.

He watches the child and the child watches him, eyes locked, both sets of eyes silvery in the eerie shifting light.

Clair speaks. "My father used to have a crow...a PET crow... her name was Phylis...before I was born. My father says crows are smarter than people."

"That's GARBAGE!"

Clair leans down and spits on her hem. "That makes em smarter than ANYTHING!" she simpers.

"Crows ain't smarter than people!" he hollers. His eyes flutter behind his glasses.

"At least AS smart as."

"THAT is pretty silly. Crows can't INVENT stuff!"

"My father says Phylis said TWENTY words." She smiles. She draws the hem of her gown up and wipes the child's crusty nose with the place she has wetted with spit. The man glares at her long freckled legs and the child pushing its face up into the wetness of the gown.

Jordan's truck retreats, becomes a far-off buzz. Then the sighing of the storm, the croaky TV in the other room, and the sick child breathing noisily through its open mouth all seem like a kind of silence.

"Maybe it was thirty words," Clair says. "I'm not sure EXACTLY."

Crowe laughs nervously. "THIRTY words ain't much."

"Well...in the past three weeks Jordan's said THREE words to me," she whispers. She gives the child a long kiss on its mouth and the child presses its heat, its hard belly and fingers up.

"Shit!" snarls the tranny man. His face is suddenly glassy with tears. "You can't win an argument with a fuckin woman . . . Jesus fuckin Christ!" He flies at her and takes up her big shoulder in both blackened hands. The storm gives the old house a furious shake.

"You are such a BITCH. You an them brats make me wanna puke."

The child closes its hand around the tranny man's thumb.

"He likes you!" Clair chirps. "Baby likes Crowe."

Crowe makes a sound in his chest like drawing up spit. Slowly Clair turns her face up at him. The smell of her old gown, too many hours of sleep, her forever-filled almost leathery breasts, the smell and the SOLIDNESS of the smell flattens over his face. The two kids from the front room reappear with mangled-looking mouths. Clair knows it's only grape jelly, or maybe Jello powder, one of their raids. But MANGLED is how it really looks. The tranny man's eyes zero in on those mouths. He rips his hands free of Clair, kicks the wee sporty cars, the fire engine, the cop cruiser. He springs at the back door, tearing it open as if to tear it off.

But there is NO OUTDOORS.

There's only the hard-packed bluish wall of snow Jordan Letourneau has plowed up there flush with the door. So Crowe just stands there looking surprised.

Clair shouts: "Well, LOOK AT THAT, AYE! Look what Daddy's gone and done to us! Blocked our door up!!! Now HOW're we EVER gonna get out?"

The tranny man lays his face lovingly against the wall of snow. His arms ripple around him as if to comfort himself. His words are only turkey gobbles against his sleeve. "Ga-gawww . . . G . . .

Goddam it . . . g . . . Goddam fuckin FIRE. God DAM. Why me!! Jesus FUCKIN Christ . . . why me?'' Then come the hard sobs of grief.

The children giggle wildly.

THE ICE FISH

Willis Johnson

Maxim Maximovich, the father of the Russian colony in Plankton, was an educated man. He did not in the least believe that Father Vladimir, the priest of the Holy Virgin of Kazan, the church in the old icehouse shed down by the river, was a spy.

Maxim Maximovich had a real estate business in town. It had been his advertisements in the Russian newspapers in New York and San Francisco that had brought the first Russian families to Plankton. This was the reason he was known as the colony's "father." He sometimes introduced himself that way, trying to say it modestly, but you could see he was proud. His wife, the baroness, who owned the Hotel Nicholas the Second, the boarding house where many of the older Russians lived, was proud, too.

The hotel once had been the home of a sea captain whose schooner had carried to Florida and the West Indies the blocks of ice cut from the river at the foot of the hill. Maxim Maximovich and the baroness lived with their daughter Sonya on the top floor.

On the roof was a cupola and a widow's walk with an iron railing wrought with stars and eagles. On summer evenings Maxim Maximovich and the baroness liked to sit out there sipping tea and gazing down upon the town and the river and the woods all around. Below them on quiet nights they could hear the chairs creaking on the veranda and they took pleasure in knowing that the old people, their fellow Russians, were out enjoying the same soft breeze, the very same sky filled with stars.

In their living room was a bookcase filled to the ceiling with books. There were books in Russian and English and some in French and German. In the bathroom was a rack of magazines that told about the stock market, movie stars, rich Arabs and what the President and other famous people had done the previous week —so that whatever important was happening in the world, Maxim Maximovich was sure to know about it.

So when people like Sergei Andreyevich Palchinsky, the president of the local chapter of the Union of True Russians, said to him about Father Vladimir, "It's not just something people sucked out of their fingers," Maxim Maximovich might nod or shake his head and appear to agree that it was an awful thing. But of course he knew better.

To him, Father Vladimir was simply an old man, a little feeble-minded, a little set in his ways. But to imply or to say outright, as did Mr. Palchinsky and many other members of Maxim Maximovich's church, the Church of Vasily the Blessed, that he was a Soviet agent ... well, Maxim Maximovich had to laugh.

Mr. Palchinsky was the warden of Vasily the Blessed. While Father Vladimir's church belonged to a branch of Russian Orthodoxy that acknowledged the legitimacy of the patriarchate of

Moscow, Vasily the Blessed belonged to the Holy Russian Church Outside of Russia, the church in exile. It didn't recognize the patriarch or anything about the Soviet Union. Its members did not even like to say the words, "Soviet Union."

As a young man, Mr. Palchinsky had fought in the Civil War against the Reds. One day in a battle a bullet had come along and clipped off the end of his nose. All he had left was a nub with nostrils that whistled slightly when he talked, so that he sounded as if he were accompanying himself on a little flute. This experience, of being shot in his nose, had left him with a terrible tremor. When he collected the offering in church on Sunday he sounded like a gypsy with a tambourine.

"He keeps a short-wave radio in his house — did you know that?" Mr. Palchinsky would say, putting his hands in his coat pockets which then would flap like small wings. " ... a radio with a long antenna."

"I've never seen it."

"You don't think he's going to leave it out for you to see, do you?"

"What are you trying to say?"

"Do you know the kinds of places you can listen to with such a big antenna?"

"What kinds?" Maxim Maximovich knew exactly what was coming.

"Why ask? You know."

"No, I don't. Why don't you say it?"

"You don't need me to say it."

"Moscow, I suppose. Havana?"

"See? And you pretend not to know."

Then Mr. Palchinsky would remind him how Gregor Miron-ovich Smolnov, who worked in the kitchen of Maxim Maxi-movich's own hotel, had heard about a priest in a Displaced Persons camp after the war who was a *seksoty* — a Soviet informer. Was it just a coincidence that this priest, by all descriptions, should have a white beard and a bald head with a long fringe of white hair at the back of his scalp so that from the rear, it was said, he looked very much as he did from the front — just like Father Vladimir?

Maxim Maximovich knew the way the people thought. The more innocent a man appeared to be, the more they suspected he was up to something. To argue would have been like throwing peas against a stone wall.

One day early in Lent, Maxim Maximovich was in the bank for a closing on a chicken farm when he decided to pay a call on Father Vladimir. It was a cold gray day and people in the town were fasting. Maxim Maximovich watched them leaning grimly into the wind as they passed the bank window, their coat collars up, their chins tucked into their chests.

For some months he had been trying to talk the old priest into selling his house and moving into the Nicholas the Second, where he would have every comfort. The house was little more than a shack — a tiny house with a tin roof and tar shingles fastened to the river bank like a nest to a tree. From the kitchen window you could look up and down the river and across to the pine woods which lifted up the sun each morning and took the glow of its setting. That was when the idea had first struck Maxim Maximovich — at sunrise. He and the baroness had been on their way home from a party when the sun rose out of the woods and made a path of shimmering gold straight across the water to them. It had excited them very much.

Maxim Maximovich was not surprised that Father Vladimir at first did not appear eager to do it. People can grow used to misery the way they do to wrinkles.

"I know you're only thinking of my own good," the priest had said. This was in November when the ground was freezing hard. "God bless you for it. You think I'm lonely, don't you?"

The next time, Maxim Maximovich had spent almost a whole afternoon in the priest's kitchen while the old man made sugar cookies. Maxim Maximovich told about all the other Russians in town who had entrusted their homes to him. As they grew older, it became hard for them to keep up with the taxes and all the repairs, especially in winter with the high cost of heating oil, not to mention the worry. Suppose your roof caved in under the snow? Suppose you got sick or slipped on the ice and hurt your back? How long might you lie there before someone found you? And even in spring your worries didn't end because the river might flood and your sump pump could break.

Now these people lived humming a tune in his wife's hotel. They were with people their own age; in the lobby they had card tables and comfortable chairs and even a color television set.

The old priest seemed to think about this. His mouth came out in a little spout and his white eyebrows knit together, as if his face were on a draw string.

Maxim Maximovich sat back confidently. He took a cookie from the dish Father Vladimir had set out and dunked it in his tea.

And that was the only thing the priest said anything about. As if Maxim Maximovich had not come with his briefcase and contract and his plan for a good life. As if he were some lady visiting from next door.

"My wife's recipe, God rest her soul," the priest said. "I'll give it to you if you'd like, Maxim Maximovich. Does your wife like to bake?"

At that point another real estate broker might have given up. But Maxim Maximovich knew better. All he had to do was wait. When the days grew colder and the world seemed to spin more slowly and it was dark more than it was light, a comfortable place where you could be was not an easy place to turn your back on —no matter how old and stubborn you were.

Maxim Maximovich's wallet, plump with his commission, pressed pleasantly against his heart. The radiator beside him in the bank gurgled with a happy sound, like a brook. The owner of the chicken farm, a thin, nervous-acting American man with an oversized wife, shook his hand with such gratitude that Maxim Maximovich was afraid the buyer might change his mind. Except that the buyer, a Russian plumber from Brooklyn who had been mugged twice in the past year on his way to work, did exactly the same thing.

Maxim Maximovich emerged from the bank as onto a stage, stopping in the middle of the shoveled path and beaming up and down the street as if acknowledging applause on each side. His neck stretched as far as it would go, holding his head up high. With one foot in his car he paused again and, for maybe a whole minute, like a hunter with his foot up on his trophy buck, smiled up at the gray cold sky as if it were full of sunshine.

Father Vladimir was kneeling at his morning prayers. When he heard the knock he turned his ear and listened.

Sometimes it happened that when someone knocked, no one was there.

Father Vladimir suspected a devil. Everything in the universe, whether it was a creature or a season or a feeling in your heart, had its opposite component. Father Vladimir was pretty sure it had something to do with God deciding to make the world go around in a circle rather than in a square or triangular movement or just having it stand still. If God gave the world saints, He also gave it devils.

Yet Father Vladimir found it hard to abide them, even the ones who only played pranks. When he opened the door and one of them wasn't there, he was relieved but also very angry. You never knew where they were hiding or what they might do next.

He knew it was a sin to slam a door in anger. So when the knock came again, he said, "Dear me. I hope it's someone."

With whispered words like air being bled from a water pipe, Father Vladimir finished his prayer and crossed himself three times.

"Excuse me," he said. "I'd better see, just in case."

Holding up his skirts, he crossed the room to the door with watchful little steps, like a lady on a stair. The bottoms of his long winter underwear hung loosely around his thin ankles.

Instead of the devil off hiding somewhere, there in his doorway stood Maxim Maximovich, his face bright and shining like the moon.

Maxim Maximovich stamped the snow off his feet. He was smiling so broadly that you would think he was showing off a dance step that took a lot of practice.

"Maxim Maximovich! What a surprise! Do you know that only this morning I was thinking of you? Or was it yesterday? I said to myself, 'Well, I'm just going to have to have a talk with Maxim Maximovich.' I think it was this morning, but never mind. Come in, come in. How's your dear wife? I want to show you something."

"I can't stay long," Maxim Maximovich said. "How are you? It's an awful day — again."

"Thanks to your prayers, I'm fine."

"The discouraging thing is that the winter's not yet halfway through." Maxim Maximovich gave a shudder, although the house was warm. In a corner a wood stove was tinged with red. A pot of water was boiling on it, its rim wearing a hoary crust like an old man's beard.

Father Vladimir carried Maxim Maximovich's coat off to the closet with both arms. He gave a grunt as he hung it up, as if it were a side of beef he was hoisting onto a hook.

"They say we're in for another good storm," Maxim Maximovich said, rubbing his hands over the stove.

'Do you think so?" Father Vladimir said, emerging from the closet. "I love the snow. Just think, all those little flakes, every one perfect. To tell you the truth, I prefer the cold to the hot. I think it has something to do with Russian blood being thicker or thinner — whichever it is. In New Jersey where we lived you could hardly breathe in summer. Olga — God give her rest — would carry the electric fan with her from room to room, wherever she went. Have you been to New Jersey? We had a nice apartment there. But the heat in summer wasn't good for us. The air was so thick you could hang a hatchet on it. I sometimes wonder if it wasn't the fan blowing on her all the time that made Olga sick."

"All I can say," said Maxim Maximovich, "is that I'm very concerned about what this cold weather does to the heating bills of our senior citizens."

"It must be hard on them, poor things," Father Vladimir said sadly. "I wish I could do something, Maxim Maximovich."

"You know, when you're a child it's different. You think winter is wonderful. On my Sonya winter produces only red cheeks. But for old people ... well, I don't have to tell you. It can be very tragic: you can get sick and even die."

"Maybe it would help," the priest said, "if I prayed for an early spring. I could start today."

"We all had better pray for something."

"That's an even better idea! Good for you, Maxim Maximovich! It may take a little time, but I'm sure God would go along if we all asked Him sincerely. Don't you think?"

"But then the people should not be counting the days," Father Vladimir added thoughtfully. "You'll have to tell them that, Maxim Maximovich: don't count. Tell them to do just as your daughter. Try to think of the ice and snow as a gift from heaven. When they see it's something wonderful they'll want it to last. But why are we standing here? You're not going already, are you? Why not stay and have a nice cup of tea? It seems like you've only just come."

Father Vladimir showed Maxim Maximovich to the kitchen table, then fell into a long silent conversation with himself, whispering in the way in which he prayed, as he fussed with the cups and spoons and paper napkins and the dish of cookies to put out. He had spent all his life studying the lives of the saints, pondering the gospels and thinking about God and what it must be like in the Kingdom of Heaven. The few practical things he knew how to do were those he had learned from his late wife. While the slats dropped out of the shutters and the porch step wobbled and the chimney leaned over a bit more each year, on the inside the house was as tidy as a widow's room. The pans and cookie sheets over the stove gleamed like a wall of mirrors. The curtains smelled fresh from the wash. Every day he dusted the tops of everything, making a needle of the rag to get in all the tiny crevices in Olga's knickknacks. Once a week he scoured the toilet bowl and scrubbed the kitchen floor. He ironed not only his outer garments but his underwear and stockings. In the spring he picked violets in the grass out back and set them on the window sill in the sun.

"Now what was I thinking?" he said when the tea was ready and he had come to sit beside Maxim Maximovich. He thought a minute before remembering how it was just that morning or yesterday that he had been looking out his window at the river and had started to think about something.

"Yes, it's depressing, isn't it?" said Maxim Maximovich.

He gazed out the window. The world was bleak. The wind was blowing. Clouds of snow carried over the river as if the woods were on fire. Maxim Maximovich gave a sigh. How sad, he thought, that people preferred to patch up the reality of their lives with their thin little lies to themselves rather than to look at their true, threadbare condition.

If he had one attribute, he felt, it was his ability, his willingness and yes, his courage, to turn pockets inside out, to shake the contents onto the table where things could be seen, once and for all, in plain view.

With his shiny round chin he pointed to the wood stove and said, "What do they charge for a cord nowadays?" and before the priest answered that it was ten dollars more than last year he already was nodding his head and saying, "It must be very hard on you."

"You'd better be careful with that chimney," he added. "It doesn't look safe to me. And you living all alone ..." He clicked his tongue. "What kind of a life is that?"

"People come all the time, Maxim Maximovich. Oh, there's no end of those who want a chat now and then. Did I tell you who came to see me last week? Try to guess."

Maxim Maximovich frowned. "I know what you're doing," he said. "Don't you know what you're doing?"

Father Vladimir looked down at himself to see if he was doing something.

"You're trying to avoid the subject."

"No, I'm not, Maxim Maximovich." After a moment, he said, "So, how's your family?"

"The subject," said Maxim Maximovich determinedly, "is your condition — your *real* condition. What can the church be paying you?"

"Well, it varies."

"I don't want to go into it," Maxim Maximovich said. "I only ask to prove a point. The point being, it's not easy to get through a winter even if you do get paid regularly. I know you don't want to talk about this, but I'm going to make you. Sooner or later you have to face it."

Father Vladimir looked into his tea cup. "A priest doesn't

need much," he murmured.

"I wouldn't worry," Maxim Maximovich said with a softened voice, " ... if only you'd learn to look out for your own interest."

Maxim Maximovich then spoke very persuasively, he thought, about his plan for Father Vladimir, pointing out how the room and board could be deducted automatically from the priest's Social Security check or other pension, so he would not even have to worry about that. Each resident of the hotel was entitled to two meals a day, breakfast and lunch. You could also have supper, but that was extra.

"There's always someone to talk to. You can play cards. You can sit on the porch and watch everything that goes on. You can reminisce ..."

"I don't like to do that, Maxim Maximovich. There's too much about the past that makes me sad ..."

"You don't have to do it," Maxim Maximovich hurried to say. "Only if you want to. Some people like to do it. It's only a suggestion."

"... Russia, my poor mother — she had such a hard life. And my Olga ... we never had any children, you know."

"You can watch television," Maxim Maximovich said. "Up on the hill we get Portland and Bangor both."

"Can you get *Little House on the Prairie*?" Father Vladimir asked.

"I don't know. I can find out. I'm pretty sure we can."

"How about *Fantasy Island*?"

"That, too," Maxim Maximovich said. "I'm almost positive."

Father Vladimir didn't say anything for a long while.

Then he said, "Imagine that ... Portland *and* Bangor."

The ladies and gentlemen of the Union of True Russians of Plankton, Maine, settled themselves onto the divan and the soft chairs in the baroness' living room and the maid brought out the Napoleon torte to go with their tea. The torte was wonderful and creamy and they all took a second helping except for Mrs. Bukharin who was fatter than some of the others and said she was on a diet. When they were done they set down their dishes and patted their napkins tidily in place on their laps and the arms of their chairs.

Mr. Palchinsky called the meeting to order. Mrs. Golitsyn, recording secretary, read the minutes. Mrs. Bukharin, the treasurer, gave the financial report. Then the baroness, who was their program chairman, introduced Father Alexey, who was going to speak on the return of Juan Carlos to the Spanish throne, an event which had much excited the members. The baroness noted that Father Alexey had studied Spanish in college and had visited Mexico on vacation.

Father Alexey was sitting at the head of the tea table. He had his legs crossed as if he were relaxed, but you could see he was nervous. He was drumming on his knee with his fingers and was looking around at the membership and nodding all the time as if his head were on a spring. From the wall a large portrait of the Tsar looked down with a patient expression, as if also waiting to hear what the priest had to say.

Father Alexey had the problem that he could not speak Russian so well, although he had studied it at the monastery and also had taken it for a semester in college. And while he had picked up quite a bit since taking over the parish of Vasily the Blessed a year ago, the words he knew were mostly little words or church words or words with which to comfort people in the hospital. With big words, especially words about politics, he wasn't very good. When the baroness introduced him, he sat up straight, smoothed his long reddish beard between his moist palms and said, "Man can only be glad, to have in Spain a king nowadays."

He hadn't got much beyond that when Maxim Maximovich came through the door in high spirits, as if he were on his way to a ball. He kissed his wife so loudly the ladies had to laugh. She scolded him jokingly and made them laugh more. That's why everyone liked them, they were just like regular people.

"Sorry *batiushka* — sorry," Maxim Maximovich said to the priest and tiptoed to a chair. He was tall and plump and good-looking and though he was a very important man he still was like a boy, the ladies thought — always up to pranks to make them laugh. Sitting forward the way he was now with his chin on his fingertips he looked to them like a naughty angel. "I'll be good," he said and winked to Vera Zolotnikov.

Father Alexey resumed his speech. "In Spain," he said, "not like Russia." He hadn't any notes to read from, but he had rehearsed at home. "Example. Franco long time ago ... he is saying he is not king, only working for meantime in king's house ..."

"In the palace," the baroness said to help out.

"He was regent," said Mr. Palchinsky, who knew.

" ... until he is old and dying," said Father Alexey. "After that is coming king."

"Juan Carlos," the ladies said together.

"Certain," said the priest.

Then one of the ladies said, "Do you think one could ever hope ...?" And they all seemed to sigh at once.

"Things not same," Father Alexey said. "But yes — maybe hope. Everybody's prayers to help, could be, could be, same is happening in Russia but I think no."

"But it's not inconceivable," the baroness said.

"Oh, wouldn't it be nice?" the lady who had asked said dreamily.

This idea led the company to speculate over who might become Tsar if the Communists got kicked out sometime soon: Grand Duke Vladimir, who was the Romanov pretender, or somebody else. The vote was in favor of somebody else, after the baroness pointed out that the Grand Duke's mother-in-law by his second marriage was Jewish.

"Then it's impossible," the members agreed.

Someone thought of Grand Duke Alexander Mikhailovich. Others also were mentioned but they were farther away from the Romanov bloodline.

They all looked despondent. Mrs. Golitsyn thought they should go on record favoring someone but Vera Zolotnikov said what if the thing about Grand Duke Vladimir's mother-in-law by his second marriage wasn't true, or maybe she had converted ... "How would we look then, our chapter?"

The members went along with Mrs. Bukharin's motion to postpone the vote until the April meeting.

All this time, Maxim Maximovich was waiting. He couldn't repress his spirits any longer. "All done?" he asked when the vote to postpone the vote was counted. "Then let's have a party!"

He took out his billfold filled with the money from the bank and showed it around the room, holding it the way you'd hold a bird, so you wouldn't hurt it.

"Here's the kind of day it's been for me," he said proudly.

Maxim Maximovich didn't say anything about Father Vladimir's house. But he let the company know that no sooner had he closed the deal in the bank than he had another desirable property ready to sign. At first glance the new listing might not seem much of a place but as people often told him, he said, he had an uncanny ability to "look into the water" and see what others could not.

When he looked at the old priest's house, as he had that first morning coming home from the party and as he had again today, looking back from his car as he drove away, he did not see just a little tin-roofed house. What he saw was the wide river and the rise of the land and the sun on the water in summer as the tourist boat steamed up river from Bath. He saw the mooring you could have, and the restaurant and gift shop. Some of the hotel's residents were clever with their hands. They could make all sorts of embroidery and other Russian things that tourists would like to buy. And what was a house but boards and shingles? You could pull out the nails and pile the whole thing up in a day.

That was what a man with vision could see. But he did not say this, either.

When lunch was ready, the company moved into the dining room where the maid, Lisaveta Stepanova, had set the long table with the dishes which her husband, Smolnov the dishwasher, had brought up from the hotel kitchen. There were potato and sauerkraut pastries, pickled mushrooms, beet salad, a tureen of hot borscht, eggplant caviar, stewed cucumbers. The baroness inspected everything to make certain there wasn't any meat or fish or sour cream. It was, after all, Lent. They had cheated a little with the Napoleon torte. God surely could forgive them for that. But to cheat twice in a day — that was getting into real sin.

Smolnov didn't go but stood there smiling insolently as the guests entered. He was a cantankerous old man, and no one liked him. He had a shaven head and his ears and nose were purple. Before the DP camp and before the war he had been in one of Stalin's camps. People said that more than once he had been beaten so that he almost died. Frankly, Maxim Maximovich could see why. They kept him on only because of Lisaveta Stepanova, a sweet thing and a good worker — worth ten of him. Maxim Maximovich had him run across to the drug store for a box of chocolates, just to get him out of there.

Maxim Maximovich got the vodka from the refrigerator. They drank to the Tsar, to good luck, to themselves and to the vodka before it got warm. Pretty soon they were all in a spirit to match Maxim Maximovich's.

Vera Zolotnikov sang a song. Mrs. Bukharin made a kerchief of her napkin and pretended to be a peasant girl. They traded the stories they loved to hear: how old Mrs. Florenskaya in her senility talked to her dead husband every day on the telephone; how Marietta Valentinova had hid backstage and wouldn't come out after the phonograph needle had got stuck during the grand finale of her winter ballet in the Methodist Church hall; how the Goncharov girl had run off with a Negro from the Coast Guard station, causing her mother to suffer a stroke and collapse on the living room sofa.

But when they turned to what was new, their happy mood changed. The latest things it seemed were all about aches and pains and nursing homes and who was having trouble going to the toilet and who had come to town for whose funeral and whether during their time of bereavement they had spoken to people to whom they were not speaking. It wasn't so funny.

They were getting depressed. To change the subject, the baroness thought of a suspicious new thing about Father Vladimir. She had heard he bought a whole bag of nylon string the other day in the hardware store. Everyone agreed this certainly was suspicious but they could not begin to think of why until Mr. Palchinsky said, "A whole bag full? Don't worry — it's for something then."

"The Soviets again?" Maxim Maximovich said with a smile.

The club members shook their heads and looked angry.

"Even our string," one of them said.

"Little by little, stealing what they can."

In the afternoon, Sonya came home from school. By this time, the company was quite upset with the Communists. Mrs. Golitsyn was suggesting a special meeting for a vote on who the successor to the Tsar might be, instead of waiting for April. This would show the Soviets that the Union of True Russians wasn't fooling around. At a look from her mother, Sonya dutifully shook each guest's hand, squirming her small fingers out the moment they were grasped, as if the larger hand were a trap that might hold her there. One or two of the ladies tried to make some small joke with her, asking if she had any boyfriends in school. She ran to her room without an answer or even a smile.

It grew dark long before the time for night. The baroness lit candles. Maxim Maximovich rang downstairs for wine. Throughout the afternoon the heat generated by the circle of friends had condensed on the windowpanes; now it froze on the glass in exotic patterns. Not being able to see out into the street, yet knowing that the cold winter was there, beyond the icy swirls and flowerlets, like a danger from which they were quite safe, made them feel as snug as if the candle flames glowing in the wine were warming fires.

It was now that the priest spoke. They watched the shadow and the light on his young face, and each of them was still.

"Don't make elephants out of flies," he told them. He was a little more tipsy than they had seen him be at church suppers when there was vodka under the tables.

"These things about Father Vladimir," he said. "Remember, God does not scatter us over the earth like seeds and forget about us. The earth is like a great garden. God gives us the sun, He gives us the water. And He gives us a third thing. How do you say it in Russian? The dirt from the cows and horses and chickens? You know — after it passes through? No really," he said when the club members laughed.

"This is the thing that is like sin," he said. "The strange thing is, we need it also, as much as the other. But you have to be careful. If it gets too close, it burns — your flowers, your peppers, the things in your garden will die. But when it is not too close — and not too far — all right, it is good. Do you see the meaning?"

The company nodded tentatively.

"Too close ... goodbye. But just the right distance ... look how beautiful is the garden!"

The company was silent. It was a funny thing for a priest to say, even if he was young and a little drunk.

"It's certainly something to think about," said Maxim Maximovich.

"You can see that *batiushka* has put a lot of thought into it," the baroness told her guests.

"More wine, *batiushka*?"

Father Alexey took another glass and drank it down. He turned to his hosts unsteadily and said, "Anyone who gives as much as you ... I'm sure you must be tired."

"Never mind, tired," said the baroness. "Our people here are like our children. Sometimes I worry about them so much I get a headache."

"When you follow always a road that rises — well, you're bound to get tired," Maxim Maximovich said, coming to his wife's side. "That's what we keep telling ourselves, father."

Before the priest left, the baroness wrapped one each of the sauerkraut and potato pastries in a napkin.

"In case you get hungry," she said, and slipped it into his coat pocket.

The next morning when he awoke not feeling well at all, Maxim Maximovich opened the shade and looked into a winter fog. Suddenly it had come warm: the flowers of ice had run down the windowpane and the roof was dripping. A little way off where the stores and houses hid in the fog, it was hard to know what was earth and what was air. Maxim Maximovich shut the shade and went back to bed.

They ate breakfast in their bedclothes at noon. Lisaveta Stepanova, still cleaning up from the night before, brought their juice and coffee and buttered toast. They divided the morning paper. Maxim Maximovich felt a little better. He said to his wife, "Pigeon, do we have anything we don't want? I'd like to give a little gift to Father Vladimir."

"Whatever for?" the baroness said, putting down her coffee cup.

"I don't know," he said. He had the back half of the paper and was reading the business news. "I feel sorry for him, I suppose."

"That's your trouble," she said. "You're always feeling sorry."

"It's the way I'm made, I guess," Maxim Maximovich said. After a moment he peered over the top of his reading glasses. "Don't we have some little thing?"

"I don't know, *dearest*," she said, getting impatient with him. "Look in the drawer. There's all sorts of junk."

"You pick something."

"Oh, really!"

"How should I know what to take?"

It was a bother, but eventually she found something. It was an ikon of the Madonna of Czestochowa. It had been given to them by someone who had not stopped to think that Czestochowa was not Russian but Polish — and not only Polish but Catholic.

"Are you sure?" Maxim Maximovich said. "It looks like a nice one."

"What are we going to do with it? I'm certainly not going to put it with *our* ikons."

"Well, it's up to you. I just thought it might be too nice."

Maxim Maximovich put it away in his briefcase. Then he dressed and went down through the lobby. Some of the residents, having had their lunch, were asleep in the comfortable chairs. Others were staring out into the fog. At the top of the veranda stairs, Maxim Maximovich stopped. He thought he heard a bird singing. It was a fragile sound; it seemed to be far away but he could not be sure. As he went down to his car the fog wrapped itself around him and he felt himself unseen, a safe thing to feel. But as he turned by the river and drove up the little rise to the priest's house the fog lifted. All at once, there was the sky, there was the sun.

"Ah, Maxim Maximovich," the priest greeted him at the door. "It's good to see you. And look, the sunshine! It's good to see you both."

Maxim Maximovich opened his briefcase on the kitchen table. He looked as if he were getting ready to perform a magic trick. The first thing he took out was the ikon of the Madonna of Czestochowa.

"Forgive me if I embarrass you, Maxim Maximovich," the priest said. "But you're just too good." He took the ikon into the living room and placed it on the altar table in the corner where he prayed.

"We've kept it all these years," Maxim Maximovich said.

"Well, now you'll have a cup of tea," the priest said. "I've baked some of those sugar cookies you like."

"And the good news is, we get those programs," Maxim Maximovich said. "*The Little House on the Prairie* and the other one. I checked first thing when I got back yesterday."

"That *is* good news, Maxim Maximovich."

"I don't think they can get them everywhere."

"I'm sure they can't. They're just about my favorite programs. You really should try to watch them sometime, Maxim Maximovich. I'm sure you'd like them."

Maxim Maximovich took out the contract. He put on his

glasses and looked it all over carefully, as if the words on it might have got juggled around in his briefcase.

"Here's what we were talking about yesterday," he said.

"Yesterday," Father Vladimir said. He brought the teacups to the table and he thought. "Of course!" he said. "I don't know where is my head. I forgot yesterday to show you." And he walked past the contract Maxim Maximovich was holding for him to see and he went into the shed. He returned with an armful of string.

"Nylon," he said, laying it on the table. He tested a strand with two sharp tugs to show how strong it was.

Maxim Maximovich started to read aloud from the paper he was holding.

"It's a net," said Father Vladimir. "Well, it's going to be a net. Maybe you can't tell yet."

"It's very nice," Maxim Maximovich said, trying to be patient.

"I think I can have it ready by spring. Guess what it's for."

"You tell me," Maxim Maximovich said.

"All right," the priest said. "But it's a bit of a story. Are you in a hurry?"

"Somewhat of a hurry, yes."

"Can you imagine, Maxim Maximovich, what it must be like to be a fish under the ice?" the priest said. "I was looking out of my window one day and that's what I was thinking. In summer it might not be so bad to be a fish — the water's warm and there are plenty of worms and bugs to eat. But how about in winter?"

"I can't imagine," Maxim Maximovich said dryly.

"Neither can I," said the priest. "But it must be awfully dark and cold down there. Three feet of ice and three feet of snow between you and the sky. They probably don't even know there's a sun in the heavens. They can't swim up, they can't look around. That would be the worst thing, I would think — not to be able to come up and see the world."

Maxim Maximovich looked at his watch.

"Anyhow, thinking about those poor fish reminded me about your real estate advertisements in the Russian newspaper," the priest said. "Do you remember the part about the sturgeon? Isn't it strange how these things come to you all at once?"

Maxim Maximovich squared himself in his chair.

"Father Vladimir ..."

"I loved how you described things. You have a real talent, Maxim Maximovich. Come to Plankton, Maine, you said. Snowy winters, cozy little houses, the green forest, a first-class hotel, sturgeon in the river, everything ... Just like Russia, you said."

The water was whistling in the kettle. Father Vladimir turned down the flame.

"Then I was looking out my window," he said. "And I thought, here's poor Maxim Maximovich worrying about how old people are going to survive — and out there sturgeon are swimming under our noses. Suppose we could catch one? Do you know how many roe are in one sturgeon, Maxim Maximovich? I don't either. I think there must be thousands, maybe a million. Just think if we could catch two! Do you know how much caviar that would make? I tell you, we've been living here with our arms folded."

Maxim Maximovich took off his glasses and said, "Let's be realistic."

"No one would have to worry then," the priest said. "I'm

telling you, Maxim Maximovich. You wouldn't have to worry. The old people wouldn't have to worry. The town would be rich."

He took the string of the net in his hands and showed it, holding it out as if he were offering communion.

"We'll put it across the river," he said. "God gives us everything. Maybe he'll give us a sturgeon."

"Suppose there aren't any?"

"It said so in the newspaper, Maxim Maximovich. I can show you. Have you forgotten?"

"Suppose they went away?"

"Where would they go? They wouldn't go away."

"Well, suppose they did?"

"You should have more faith, Maxim Maximovich," the priest reproached him. "Just think of what it would be like, not having to live like a fish beating against the ice. Maxim Maximovich, we're going to have a real hope now!"

Father Vladimir watched Maxim Maximovich drive away. Steam was rising from the snowy street outside his window and from the roofs and trees of the town. It was as if suddenly underneath the snow, everywhere at once, there was warmth; as if all you had to do was push back the snow and there would be the earth, already in spring.

The priest smiled. He could still see Maxim Maximovich with the sun in his eyes, his foot down on the gas, scowling like a stepchild. He could hear him saying to Sergei Palchinsky, "Well, you were right."

He had looked so comical marching out with his briefcase like a flag folded in defeat. Then all at once turning back to say it, the door usually being where you say what you had in your heart to say in the first place.

"Were you in a camp in Austria after the war? Just answer yes or no, if you don't mind."

And Father Vladimir had just smiled and said sweetly, "Three camps in all, Maxim Maximovich. Why do you ask?"

Father Vladimir closed the curtain and came back to the table. The kettle was softly whistling on the stove. People like Maxim Maximovich recovered quickly from their setbacks, he thought. In no time he would be himself again. In that case he would not be saying anything so direct to Sergei Palchinsky. He was, after all, an educated man.

It would be something ambiguous.

"Father Vladimir an informer? Well, one never knows ..."

Something like that. You didn't need much.

Father Vladimir put the net for the sturgeon away in the shed. Then he filled his teapot with the hot water and took a bite out of a cookie, smacking the sugar from his fingertips with little kisses.

SQUATTER'S RIGHTS

Fred Bonnie

As Lloyd was heating water for tea with his lunch, he heard voices outside the cabin and went to the door. He had left it ajar. Two men, one of them his son-in-law, Gordon, stood in front of the old black Chevy which had been parked by the cabin for seven years. Gordon glanced toward the cabin door, saw the old man peeking, and looked away. He fished in his pocket. "I got the key in here somewheres...."

"You mean this thing runs?" the other man chided.

Gordon said nothing. He opened the door and slid in. The car started effortlessly, as if sitting behind the wheel were enough to spark the ignition. Gordon got out and both men stepped back from the car to look at it. It was covered with leaves and the two front tires were flat, but the engine hummed like the August evening insects.

"Don't sound bad," the visitor said.

Lloyd looked on through the partly open door, but when the

visitor looked up and noticed him, he pushed the door shut.

"Mornin', Lloyd," the visitor hollered.

Gordon raised the hood and the leaves slid down toward the windshield. "This oil ain't been changed in two, three years and look at it. Still yellow." He pulled out the dipstick for Sid to see.

"How about those tires, though, Gordon? You gonna put a couple new tires on the front for me?"

"Hadn't planned on it."

"Well, now, I can't very well buy it if I can't even drive it home, can I?"

"Well, go get some tires," Gordon suggested. "I'll help you put them on."

"That ain't the point, Gordon." Sid scratched the back of his neck. "The point is I don't feel like forking out money for a pair of tires."

Both men were silent for a moment. Sid glanced over his shoulder at the cabin. "Say, Gordon, the old man's getting a little loose in his old age, ain't he?"

"No worse than ever."

"What does he do with himself all day?"

"I dunno," Gordon said, his eyes on the car. "Just sits, I guess."

Lloyd backed away from the door, then took a rusted double-barrelled shotgun from a wall cabinet. He opened it and stuffed a plastic pill vial into one of the barrels, then shut it again.

"Hey, Lloyd," he heard Sid holler. "Come on out and say hello. Ain't seen you in years."

Lloyd slid along the wall to the window and peeped outside until Sid turned back to the car. Lloyd raised the shotgun and took aim. Bam, he whispered.

He lowered the gun and watched as the two men shut the hood and sauntered off. Then he went out to the car and inspected it, shotgun still in hand. What could he take, he wondered, to prevent their driving that car off? A few spark plugs. But Gordon probably had spark plugs right up there in the barn. And if he didn't, they could always get some at a filling station.

He could take the distributor cap. They would have to look around a little before they would find a 1949 Chevy distributor cap. Then they'd have to look around for a generator too....

Gordon and Sid came back after lunch carrying tires, windshield wiper blades and a seat cover. Lloyd watched through a peephole he had drilled in the door for the occasion. By the time they had changed the tires it was after two o'clock and the sky had darkened. Lloyd watched the spasms of breeze lift the leaves from the car, hold them for a moment, then twist them away.

"Looks like we're gonna get that storm," Sid said.

"A-yuh."

Gordon slid behind the wheel and tried to start the car. Listening to the unconvinced churning of the engine, he turned toward the cabin.

"What's the matter?" Sid asked. "She started all right this forenoon."

Gordon lifted the hood and his eyes roamed over the engine. "That old lizard," he muttered. He turned toward the cabin. "Okay Lloyd, you can bring that generator and distributor cap out any time, along with anything else you took."

No response.

"Damn it, you bring that stuff out here!"

"I threw it out," Lloyd hollered through the barred door. "Distributor cap warn't no good. Inside was all coated with cow dung."

Gordon and Sid looked at each other.

"Just bring it out," Gordon hollered. "We'll worry about the cowshit."

"Too late now," Lloyd said. "It's gone. Used it for fertilizer."

Gordon strode onto the porch and tried to open the door. "C'mon, Lloyd. This ain't the time for games."

Lloyd's voice rose high and strained. "Well now, if you'd asked me one time what I thought about you selling my car, perhaps we wouldn't be playing them."

"That happens to be my car," Gordon said, his eyes focused on the latch. "Besides, you ain't driven it in ten years."

"I asked you over eight years ago for that car and you didn't say no. It's mine now. Been here over seven years. Squatter's rights."

"Well, let me inside. We can talk about it."

"It ain't for sale," Lloyd said. "There ain't nothing to talk about."

"Don't forget," Gordon said, talking more quietly now. "The court appointed Bertha and me to be your legal guardians. I wouldn't have to ask you about selling that car."

"That car ain't gettin' sold," Lloyd said.

Gordon waited just a second before taking up the challenge. "It ain't, huh? We'll see." He came back to the car where Sid waited. "Look, Joe Duffy has a junk Chevy over in his backyard. I'll zip over there and get the distributor cap and generator off'n it. You stay here and make sure he don't do anything more."

"I ain't got all afternoon, Gordon. This storm's gonna get

worse and worse."

"I'll be back in a few minutes," Gordon said. He stuffed his pipe into his breast pocket, stem first. The wind licked at the wisps of hair sticking out under his hat.

Sid turned back toward the cabin, certain that Lloyd was watching him. "Whatcha been up to, Lloyd?" he hollered. He glanced from window to window, uncomfortable with the old man so close but not in sight. He opened the car door and got in. There were no longer leaves on the windshield and Sid noticed that it was cracked in one place. He could still get an inspection sticker though, he thought. His eye caught the tongues of wind that dipped into the tall meadow grasses and he thought about his cows waiting, probably, at the pasture gate to be let into the barn. He hoped someone would get home soon to let them in.

When he looked up at the cabin again, he saw half of Lloyd's face peering out at him, the other half hidden by the window frame. Sid waved once, but Lloyd neither waved back nor moved; he kept only half his face visible and pressed against the pane. Sid turned so that his back was toward the cabin but he continued to feel Lloyd's stare.

When he turned to look again, Lloyd was gone. Sid breathed on the window to fog it up in case Lloyd decided to stare at him from a different window. He watched the wind and thought of all the things, besides the cows, he had to do if there really was a hurricane coming, as the radio had warned.

By the time Gordon got back with the distributor cap, it was nearly four. Sid leaned against the fender and watched him work. Gordon cussed the wind as it blew his hair in his face.

"Say, Gordon, I thought you said the oil in this thing was

changed two years ago."

"That's right."

"Well what's the old man saying — something about he ain't drove it in seven years?"

"What have you, been talking to him while I was gone?"

"No...I hollered to him a couple of times in there but he wouldn't answer."

"Well, don't listen to him, even if he answers."

Sid watched without speaking for a few minutes more, glancing from time to time at the door of the cabin when it rattled in the stronger gusts.

"Gordon, are you sure you didn't change that oil just this morning before I came out?"

Gordon looked up. "You calling me a liar?"

"No, I was just wondering."

Gordon stood up from under the hood and held the wrench toward Sid. "Look, you can put your own generator on..."

Sid looked at the wrench but didn't take it. "I didn't mean nothing by that, Gordon. You don't hafta get mad."

Gordon bent over the engine again. Neither of them spoke until Gordon was done.

"Start her up," Gordon ordered.

Sid got in and turned the key. The motor churned but it wouldn't start. Gordon's eyes crawled over the engine from the radiator cap to the windshield wipers.

"Hey, Sid," the old man hollered from inside the cabin. "You want to buy something that don't even start?"

Sid looked at Gordon and then at the cabin. "It started okay this morning, Lloyd, and it'd prob'ly be okay now if you hadn't been messing with it."

"Yeah, but how do you know I ain't done something beyond fixing?"

"Don't listen to him," Gordon warned, pointing.

"Like, how do you know I ain't dumped a little sawdust into the gas tank?"

Sid looked automatically toward the gas cap, then down at the ground.

"Don't listen to him, I tell you. He'll lie to the preacher at his own funeral."

Sid pointed solemnly at the sawdust leavings there on the ground. "Look at that."

Gordon shrugged. "He probably sprinkled a little sawdust there just so's you'd think he'd done something more."

The hesitation grew on Sid's face.

"Course it depends," Lloyd hollered, "on just what you're lookin' for in a car. Now if you just want somethin' to sit in, this one may do. But if you're looking for something to drive, I'd look elsewhere."

"You ain't gonna believe him, are you?" Gordon pressed.

"How much you paying for it?" Lloyd asked.

"A hundred."

Lloyd laughed. "Offer him ten."

Sid looked pained.

"Awwww, go on," Gordon said disgustedly. "If you're gonna believe him you're as crazy as he is."

Sid shuffled nervously, looking up at the sky. "Look, I gotta get back and get my cows in. We can talk about it tomorrow, after the storm...."

"Awww..."

"Well, see you later..."

"Hold on a minute there, Sid. I just went out and spent two dollars on a distributor cap and five for a generator for this thing. I figure you owe me seven bucks."

Sid weighed the situation. If he paid, he wouldn't have to feel obligated to buy a car that might have sawdust in the gas tank. "Okay," he said, reaching for his wallet. "But I'll take that distributor cap and generator along with me."

After they had gone, Lloyd went out to replace the distributor cap and generator as well as the coil and several worthless spark plugs. It had begun to rain and the wind blew in wet slaps around his face. After he studied the wires under the dashboard and remembered which ones to cross, the car started easily. He wanted to leave right away, but he knew he would have to wait until nightfall to get by Gordon.

He went into the cabin and began to pack. He didn't plan to take much with him : two shirts, a radio that no longer worked, socks, underwear, two savings bonds, his old shotgun. The more he looked around the cabin, the more things he saw that he wanted to take. He piled things on the back seat of the car: clothes, tools, old magazines, a zither with no strings. He thought of Gordon and how upset he would be that the car was gone, but happy enough to be rid of Lloyd that he would not come after it. Lloyd would be happy to be rid of Gordon, too...his attempts to get Lloyd into a nursing home. Lloyd had refused to talk about it and even threatened to burn the house down if they ever brought it up again. The next day he had moved his things out of the big house and into the cabin he had built for himself back when Gordon and Bertha were first married; built it, he said, for his old age. The black Chevy had been abandoned by the cabin even before Lloyd moved.

He made a stew from leftovers in the refrigerator and ate, still thinking about Gordon and how they had argued from the beginning; Gordon coming one day to see about a tractor Lloyd had for sale and arguing with him about the horsepower. He didn't buy the tractor, but he was back the next month when Lloyd had a horse for sale. That was the first time Gordon saw Bertha. After that he started coming regularly for eggs. Bertha was flirtatious and although she wasn't really buxom, she knew how to hold her shoulders so that she seemed so. She was nineteen when they married, and Gordon was thirty-two. Within a year he was able to buy the farm which Lloyd had leased for over 30 years but which he had never been able to buy. Now Gordon milked 40 head and owned almost 300 acres of land.

The wind whistled over the chimney and shook the windows. Lloyd listened for a while, then decided it was dark enough and stormy enough for him to get by the house.

He drove with the window rolled down and the lights out, easing through the muddy cow path. The rain pelted the windshield so hard that Lloyd had to drive with his head out the window to see. He could hear nothing above the blasts of wind and he reached the road sooner than he'd expected. A few hundred yards beyond the house he turned the headlights on. He rolled the window up and wiped off his face and hair with one of his spare shirts.

He knew he had to go south to get to Florida, so he headed south. On the open road, the wind grappled with the car. He drove slowly, neck craned and nervous as he gripped the steering-wheel. The driving rain had obliterated the lane markings in the road. He had never liked to drive and hadn't really expected to ever drive again. The few friends he had came to see him every six or eight months and that was all the sociability he wanted. Any more than a few people at a time made him nervous. Bertha made him nervous, too, when she came to sit and talk about the curtains she was going to make for him and the braided rug she'd been working on for over a year. Bertha had evolved from almost buxom to plump in eighteen years of childless marriage.

The driving was a little easier once he got onto the main road. The road was wider and the lane markings were visible, although just barely. When he rolled up his window, the hiss of the tires on the flowing pavement became inseparable from the noises of the car; the rattles from under the dashboard, the warped blade in the heater fan which tinkled against the grille. He turned on the radio and listened to the static. He thought of the two dogs he'd lost to hunters and the one dog he'd had to shoot himself after the dog got rabies and bit one of Gordon's cows.

Lloyd hit a deep rut and the impact jarred the hood latch loose. The hood rose, hesitated a moment, then snapped off the hinges and clattered over the roof into the road behind him. He wasn't sure what to do, so he pulled over to the side of the road. The next gust of wind tossed the hood into the gully. In moments the engine stalled and Lloyd couldn't get it started again. The rain battered the roof and swept in a thick film down the windshield. He opened the window and stuck his head out. At first the rain felt good against his cheek, collecting in his week-old whiskers. But as the water began to run down his neck, it gave him a chill and he closed his window again.

He remembered a can of sardines he had packed and began to search for it. He had brought a box of crackers, too, and apples from the tree behind his cabin. He ate sardines until he was full, then waited a while before eating an apple. As he smoked a cigarette, he thought he saw headlights in the thick rain on his windshield. As the car passed, Lloyd saw that it was a police car. The man inside looked over at him. Lloyd watched the blurred form pull over in back of him. He rolled his window tight and locked all the doors. In a moment the officer tapped with his flashlight on the window. Lloyd stared straight ahead.

"Hey in there, you all right?"

Lloyd nodded.

"You got new plates for this vehicle?" the officer asked.

Lloyd didn't answer.

"Get out your license and registration and come on back to my car," the officer said.

"Left them at home," Lloyd said.

The officer's powerful flashlight roamed over the car, hovering for a moment over the exposed engine, then beaming directly in on Lloyd. "The plates on this vehicle expired seven years ago." He tried to open Lloyd's door, then the back door. "Open up."

Lloyd stared straight ahead.

"This is no time for games, old fella."

Lloyd made no move to open the door and continued to stare straight ahead. The officer went back to his car and turned on the blue light. Lloyd watched the light swirl in his rear-view mirror. He tried to start the car again but everything was too wet. In a few minutes the flashlight tapped again.

"Are you Gordon Burgess?"

By instinct Lloyd shook his head.

"Then who are you?"

No reply.

"Look fella, I could arrest you right now for driving an unregistered, uninspected vehicle, probably driving without a license, refusing to co-operate with an officer, and parking so as to obstruct a throughway. And if you don't open the door and tell me who you are, I'm adding resisting arrest and stealing a car to the list."

"This is my car," Lloyd jumped, turning to face the man.

"The last registration on this car was under the name Gordon Burgess. If that isn't you, you're liable for car theft."

"Okay, okay, I'm Gordon Burgess." Lloyd swallowed hard as he said it.

"I think you're lying," the officer said.

"Why don't you go prevent a murder some place and leave me the hell alone," Lloyd exploded into the beam of the officer's flashlight. The officer said nothing and went back to his car. At first Lloyd thought he was going to leave, but he didn't. The blue light continued to turn through the thick rain on Lloyd's back window.

When Lloyd saw a new set of headlights approaching, he knew it was Gordon. The blue light continued to turn. Lloyd tried the engine again. He looked at the back seat piled high with his things, then Gordon and the officer were at his window.

"Open it up, Lloyd. Before you get in any more trouble than

you already are."

"Leave me alone."

"Want me to press charges against you for car theft?"

"Go ahead. It's my car."

Gordon took out his key and fumbled with it, inserting it finally in the lock, but Lloyd pressed with the bottom of his fist on the inside lock button. The button strained but did not come up. Gordon took the key out and ran to the other side of the car, but Lloyd held that button down, too.

Gordon cussed, then said to the officer, "Come here a minute."

Lloyd watched them go to the back of the Chevy and crouch out of sight behind it. Lloyd slid to the middle of the seat and stretched his arms to reach both lock buttons. He was able to reach them with his fingertips, but not with his fists. Instead, he lay on his back across the seat and held one button with his heel and the other with his hands. There were no exterior locks on the back doors. As he suspected, they came to both sides of the car and both had keys, though only one, Lloyd figured, was the Chevy key. They stayed crouched out of sight, but Lloyd knew Gordon was on the driver's side; he could feel him through the door.

The real key was on the other side, he could tell in his heel. He sprang to it with both hands, realizing he was staking everything on Gordon's having only one key to the Chevy. The officer turned hard and the key snapped off inside the lock.

"Oh no," Gordon groaned. He grabbed the door handle and rocked the car violently. "So help me, I'll take that door right off the hinges if you don't open up."

Lloyd plugged his ears and stared straight ahead.

Gordon and the officer went back to the patrol car. The inside light was on and in the subsiding rain Lloyd could see them talking. He waited for them to come back but they didn't. He decided to eat some more sardines and crackers. As he ate, he kept a constant eye on the patrol car. The officer was a good twenty years younger than Gordon, Lloyd could see.

When they did come back, Gordon looked calmer and stood with his hands in his pockets. "I'm trying to work out a deal for you," Gordon said. "This man here is pretty upset with you and I don't blame him a bit. Now he's suggesting that if we take you home and come back some other day to get the car, he'll forget he ever laid eyes on you, but if you don't cut this nonsense out, he's taking you in for car theft and a whole slew of other charges."

Lloyd stared straight ahead, watching the windshield wipers where they had frozen in mid-act. Without the heater the car was cold.

"We'll give you two minutes to decide, Lloyd. Just come on over and get in when you're ready."

They went back to the patrol car. The officer turned off his blue light and turned on the yellow flashers.

The two minutes went by quickly. Lloyd counted silently to 120, then waited for the yellow flashers to go off and the blue light to come back on. He noticed that the rain was letting up but the wind still shook the car from time to time. He tried to start the engine once more.

A new flashing yellow light appeared in the mirror and a wrecker pulled up to the patrol car. Lloyd saw Gordon motion with his thumb at the Chevy.

Lloyd sat straight up as the wrecker pulled in front of him, then backed up quickly. Lloyd grabbed the steering wheel to brace himself, but the wrecker did not ram him. Lloyd looked in the mirror and saw that Gordon and the officer were still in the patrol car.

The wrecker operator jumped out and disappeared under the front of Lloyd's car. Lloyd heard the chains latch like handcuffs onto the front end. Moments later, the winch jerked the front of the car off the ground. Through his windshield Lloyd could see only the top of the winch. The operator unhooked the linkage arm from the shifting lever, then disengaged the gears. Lloyd yanked at the handbrake but remembered the cable had rotted out years before. The wrecker lurched forward and Lloyd nearly smacked his head on the windshield. Behind them followed the police car with the blue light back on as well as the yellow flashers. Behind the cruiser came Gordon. Each time they went through a rut, the car swayed and Lloyd hugged the steering wheel. He figured he was being hauled to jail, but at the first filling station they came to, the wrecker made a U-turn and headed back toward Morrisville. Of course, he thought, they would put him in jail in Morrisville.

But they passed through the town and headed back out toward Gordon's farm rather than turning left to go toward the town hall, two rooms of which had bars on the windows and were used for a jail. The wind was more even now, though still strong, and the rain had nearly stopped. Here and there a tree had been blown over and there were new ruts in the road. They met two other cars on the outskirts of town and both drivers pulled over to let the procession by, gaping at Lloyd as he glared back at them.

At Gordon's road they stopped. All the flashing lights went off and the cruiser backed around and left. Lloyd saw Gordon pay the wrecker operator and squinted trying to see how much. When the wrecker moved again, Gordon didn't follow. He went, instead, up the hill to his house.

The wrecker towed Lloyd to his cabin and set him down in what Lloyd considered the wrong place. He rolled down the window as the operator got out. "Hey, would you set it down over there?"

The operator looked annoyed. "Come on man…"

"Look, I'll pay you. You can have the battery out of this thing — and any other parts you want."

The operator glanced at the exposed engine. "That battery's not worth the powder to blow it to hell." He sighed and started to get back into the wrecker. "Hold on."

He set the Chevy down more or less exactly where Lloyd wanted it. The sun was beginning to come up, buried deep in the clouds. Lloyd watched how fast the sky moved in the wind.

He waved at the wrecker as it pulled away and the operator waved back. Lloyd rummaged in the back seat for blankets and a pillow, then settled himself in the front seat to sleep.

JACK LIGHT AND MISS TEENAGE MAINE
Dan Domench

Where He Is

Four story dormitory. University of Maine at Farmington. June. I'm the man in charge of the residents. At breakfast my boss tells me to watch for a new arrival. On the way back to my room, as I come up the front walk, a strange voice yells from the second floor shower window, Vacationland!

A Natural Man

Naked and wet walking down the second floor hallway, wild curly hair, his towel around his neck like a scarf, round belly, round shoulders, hairless chest, his penis bounces happily.

Hey, I tell him, this is a coed floor. His blue eyes roll skyward, and he says, my God, what was I thinking?... Coeds! He brings the towel to his waist, drying himself a little, in no hurry.

Reasons to Travel

My name's Jack Light, glad to meet you, born in D.C., from there to London and Germany, now discharged from the Air Force. London, what a place. Look at these photos. See that one there. Are you seeing her? She wasn't that short actually. She's standing in a hole or something... You know, I think she's in the U.S.A. searching for me. I do. But she'd never look in Maine. They never heard of Maine in London.

What His Daddy Likes

Air traffic control is what he wants me to be. I liked the stewardess idea, hanging around the lounges, but they don't have a stewardess system in the Air Force. Besides I like Weather. Especially night shift. Have a few pops and watch the radar. Make some phone calls. My Dad encourages me to be what I have to be. I want him to buy a hotel in Wiscasset. He's got money from stocks. I'll manage it for him. Sit at the desk all night. Help them carry their luggage in. The women.

His Mother's Eyes

She may show up here. She travels at night. I'm not kidding. She's short, stocky with curly white hair and black huge glasses, the fashionable kind. If you see my mother at the door, you holler at me. Give me a few minutes to straighten up. She's crazy. She thinks I can't live without a maid.

Our Natural Resources

My family's not from Maine, like I said. But I love this state. I feel like I grew up here. We summered every summer at Sebago Lake. Oh man, those french girls!

He Hits The Books

Computer Science is the only major anymore. I want that degree and I'm here to learn, man. The service has matured me. I'm studying up the yin yang.

Practical Math

Number one is tell me about the librarian girl. I was unloading my luggage. It was a great morning, the sky was full of low cumulus and I saw her walk into the library. I followed her. She sat behind the counter. I gave her a look. She gave a look back. Then an old lady came over and I left. Listen, who is she? How can I get to her tonight? You must know who I mean, she's tall and has tits as big as your head.

The Moral Stand Of The Native

I tell him, the librarian's a good person, from Presque Isle. Religious. I'm not going to help you date women. You try what you want. It's a free country.

He says, you Mainers keep to yourselves, don't you?

A Series Of Romantic Cuts

Arriving for work, Jack Light is there opening the door for her. Surprise, he brings her lunch. They stroll around the campus, birds singing. He makes eye contact, often. He phones her at work and tells her to look out the window at the sunset. He waits for her at quitting time. They drive in the summer evening. He turns the radio up.

Activism On A National Scale

I return to the dorm at midnight. I have been stuffing envelopes for the Nuclear Freeze. I hear the librarian giggling in Jack Light's room. I hear Jack. He is talking about bookstores, a chain of them coast to coast.

The Private Sector

Accountants from The Augusta Executive Training Club convene on campus. Jack Light greets the arrivals, helps them find their rooms. He is particularly helpful to a petite bespectacled CPA from Waterville. He invites her to four o'clock tea in his room. He talks equity, and tax shelters. The door closes.

She leaves his room at five o'clock, glasses in her purse. She passes the librarian at the door as she steps outside. The librarian enters. Jack Light walks into the hallway wearing only tennis shorts. When he sees the librarian approaching he calls out, ice cream! dinner in town! a drive in my car!

He Incorporates Dancing

Jack Light redecorates Buddy Sanford's room: liquor area, soft lights, a small phonograph. Why not, says Buddy Sanford, who is a nice guy. Every night on the second floor, there is a dance party. It is quiet and sophisticated. Girls from town are invited. Sometimes Jack Light disappears to his room for fifteen to twenty minutes, but he comes right back.

Physics

The librarian doesn't know the accountant who doesn't know the waitress who doesn't care about the laundry girl anyway.

Traffic Flow

Afternoon. Aerial view. The librarian drives up and stops. The freshly-showered accountant gets in her car and drives off. The waitress pedals her ten-speed through the lot and looks up at the dorm. I step back a little in the window. Jack Light is parked down there, in a van, talking condominiums with a girl from Kennebunkport. Glasses clink from Buddy Sanford's room as he straightens up for the evening. The van drives off leaving Jack Light standing in the center of the lot. Cars come and go. His tennis shorts are on backwards.

Agriculture

The Maine State Antique Doll Show rents the soccer field. Jack Light walks from table to table, the self-appointed host of the campus. He is getting heavier. He pats his belly. A girl from Aroostook County picks up one of her dolls and tells him, you should see the fields when the potato blossoms bloom. He moves close, just once before I die I'd like to see that. He sighs, tell me, when's the last time someone took you dancing?

Deregulation

My boss tells me at breakfast, the first floor will be 30 high school music camp girls, you keep the second floor as it is, the third floor will be 107 Elder Hostel senior citizens, the fourth floor will be 36 Miss Teenage Maine contestants, you foresee any problems?

Venture Capital, Marketing, and Breakout

Buddy Sanford and the waitress set up a buffet table in the hall: ham, cheese, dip, and french bread. Elvis sings on the phonograph in the room, next to the tub of soda pop on ice. As I walk by Buddy says, Jack Light's idea — a hospitality suite for the teens.

I grab my backpack, a few clothes, my shaving kit, and head for the door. Coming up the walk is my boss and Jack Light. Jack has gained thirty to forty pounds. He is red-faced and joyous. My boss looks dizzy. I step back from the door, into the shadows, and they enter. Jack Light says, a production for the people in town, for the elderly, a little music, a little Miss Teenage Maine posing, totally paid for and sponsored by a timeshare condo group in Old Orchard Beach.

They move down the hall and I step outside. On the walk I pass the librarian and the accountant walking together and the librarian says, it's only a small farm really and Grandmother's getting so old, if the liquidation would start up a couple of bookstores then I know she'd approve *eventually*, she loved books.

The accountant says, if anybody can set you up, Jack Light can.

I throw my backpack and clothes into my Nova. A bus full of teenage girls parks in front of me. They unload racks of sparkling costumes. One of them looks up at the dorm windows and says, I'd give anything to be Miss Teenage Maine. Her green eyes moisten, she could almost cry.

God Speaks Through Television

At this very moment, in Portland, Maine, in the Convention Center, a camera pans an enormous hall stuffed with hundreds of Jack Lights, male and female Jack Lights. Exuberant. Chubby. Making incredible deals that promise to bring thousands of new jobs to Maine. They pause in their eating and drinking and talking only to touch each other passionately.

THE MAINE FOOD PLAN

Sanford Phippen

"The ugliest couple in the world," my father called Pean and Minerva. "The goddamned ugliest" he'd ever seen; and it was true that standing side by side they did make the man and woman in *American Gothic* look positively cheerful and light-hearted.

"They can't help it," my mother would say, "and they *are* relatives, remember."

"That's just the problem," my father would explain, "we can't get away from 'em."

But growing up I don't remember ever having much to do with Uncle Pean, whose real name was Abner, and Aunt Minerva, even though they lived right across the road at my great-grandfather's place.

Since we didn't get indoor plumbing until the mid-1950's, we had to get our water every day from their well; and it was my job as well as my older brother's to keep the pails, washtub, and water bottles in the kitchen pantry and cellarway filled. Sometimes, when I'd be filling up a pail from the well, Pean would be lurking there warning me about the big black snakes that inhabited the well. I'd peer down as far as I could, but while I could see the water, I never saw any snakes swimming around.

Pean always seemed to be lurking or slouching about because he evidently couldn't stand up straight. He was hunched over because of some debilitating disease, and wore an old cap pulled down almost over his eyes. He had a big hooked nose, always sported a stubble of beard, and usually had a cigarette hanging out of his mouth. He wore filthy overcoats that were too big for him, and muddy clamming boots, because what he did for a living was go clamming.

That day when Pean told me about the snakes, I pulled my ten-year-old head back out of the well after a second long look and said, "Pean, I don't see any snakes down there."

"You can't see 'em," he said, standing there in his hat and overcoat puffing on his cigarette, hunched over above me against the sky. "They're blacker than hell, for Christ's sake, and they're way down in the water. The only way you can see 'em is if they crawl into your pail when you're hauling it up."

So after that explanation, I hauled every pail up very slowly and got a good look in it before I brought it all the way to the top of the well. Some nights my mother would make me run across the road to get a pail of water, and I'd take a flashlight with me; but even flashing the light down in and around the sides of the well, I still never saw any snakes.

But I'd always see Pean going with the tides, coming and going from down the shore road with his clam hoe and hod. He never seemed to dig many clams, only a hodful at a time; but he and

Minerva would shuck them out, put them in glass jars, and sell them to us and the other neighbors. Before I knew better, I used to think that Pean was all bent over from clam-digging for so many years.

If we were having clams for supper, my mother used to warn my brother and me not to tell our father that the clams were from Pean, because he would always say that clams shucked out by Pean were unfit to eat. One time I asked my father why Uncle Abner was called Pean, and my father said, "Look at him. If that isn't a *Pean*, what is it? He looks just like a *pean* to me."

Sometimes Pean would motion for me to come over across the road up his clamshell driveway to his back kitchen door where he would give me some boxtops he'd saved.

"You can trade 'em in," he'd say.

"You have to send some money in with 'em!" I'd say.

"That's right, you'll need some money," he'd say; but he never said anything about giving me any.

Minerva was a case. Before she married Pean, she had been a schoolteacher in the days when a person could start teaching with only a high school diploma. Minerva always tried to be very nice to me, Cousin Lillie Partridge, and the other neighborhood kids. She would coo and goo and crouch down to us, asking us if we liked school and if we were having a good day and so on; but she was such a homely-looking creature, especially with her face all contorted and twisted into the clown face that she thought would amuse children. Instead, she scared the hell out of us. She had big lips, bug eyes, bad breath, a mustache, and always wore hair nets. When I was growing up, Minerva taught Sunday school, but at the Baptist Church, not the Congregational, where I went. I'd hear her, though, sometimes out back of her house in her garden, or just walking down the road, singing and humming her hymns. Sunday mornings we'd see her all dressed up with her navy blue hat with the white feather in it, standing by the road clutching her Bible in her white-gloved hands waiting for another Baptist stalwart to pick her up.

Pean and Minerva only lived in the back of great-grandfather's house. The front part belonged to Pean's brother Allard and his wife Myra, who lived in Bangor most of the time; but some weekends, especially during warm weather, they'd come down and stay. The two couples, however, never got along very well. Allard and Myra would always sit for hours out on their front porch together, but I don't ever remember Pean and Minerva joining them.

When I was very young, about five years old or so, I remember Aunt Carrie, Pean's and Allard's mother, lived across the road, too. In the summers Carrie moved from the main house into her little summer house, really just a shack, which sat in a field adjacent to my great-grandfather's apple orchard. I remember Cousin Lillie and me interrupting our play to run over and see Aunt Carrie, who would be resting on her glider on the porch of the summer house. She seemed very, very old to us, with deeply-wrinkled skin and bony hands and shoulders, but she was always smiling and very friendly. We'd take her wildflowers and homemade cookies from my mother and sit with her on the glider, gliding back and forth while she told us stories from her past.

Aunt Carrie's death was the first I ever remember. Lillie and I were coming home from school, which was just down the road, one afternoon, when we saw this long line of strange cars in front of Pean's house. We hadn't been told. We didn't even know Aunt

Carrie had been sick. And it had been decided by our elders that we weren't to attend her funeral. It was a shock to see everyone dressed in black and dark colors and to see Pean, as well as other male relatives, dressed in a suit. We were given some cookies and punch and we went around asking our relatives and neighbors many questions while trying to figure out this funeral business.

Minerva was a big one for clubs and plans. She was always getting up a club among the neighborhood women. One was the Popular Club which sent out a catalog of clothes and household items. Whoever started the club had to get ten members to agree to pay a dollar for ten weeks to get something in the club worth ten dollars. The person in charge could then order something worth thirty dollars. Minerva claimed she had furnished her house by starting all these plans. She was the first in the neighborhood back in the '50s to have a Tupperware party. She would always be scurrying around the neighborhood getting people to sign up for this and that, buying raffle tickets for some big prize, taking a chance on some drawing.

My mother would be sitting around the kitchen table with my aunts and neighbor women when Minerva would rush in with a new catalog.

"Look at this, girls! I've got the new Better Homes Club catalog. How many turns do you want to take, Bunny?"

Well, let me see the catalog first," said Aunt Bunny, "to see if they've got anything I'd want."

"I hope I can get you all to belong to this one," said Minerva, "because I've got to get some new bedding."

"Yeah, Pean looks like he could use some new bedding," Bunny said, grinning at the other ladies.

Then, there was the Maine Food Plan, a grand scheme whereby a customer would agree to pay so much a month for a new freezer which would be stocked by the Maine Food company according to how much you paid per month. There were several variations on the plan. Minerva and Pean signed up right away for it, and we all went over to their house when the new freezer was installed to see it and the various types of meat they received in the first shipment.

Minerva fast became the Plan's most ardent spokesman. She'd take packages of the meat around from house to house to show people and tell them how great it was.

"Pean and I have never eaten better," she declared.

Minerva did convince a few people up and down the road to belong to the plan, but she had a hard time trying to get my father to sign up.

"First of all," he told her, "I don't like the taste of frozen meat. And, second, when I get a deer in the fall, that goes us most of the winter, and I'd take deer meat anytime over frozen beef or pork."

"But you do get such nice variety," explained Minerva.

"Yeah, from what I'm told, they start out by giving you the good stuff, a good piece of steak, then the next shipment you're down to stew meat, and finally a bag of hooves! I think it's all a crooked scheme by the meat companies to get rid of their gristly odds and ends. It doesn't make any economic sense, Minerva."

It was only a year or so after Minerva and Pean had been living on the Maine Food Plan that Pean died.

I remember overhearing my mother and aunts in the kitchen talking about it.

"They took him up to Bangor and opened him up and he was full of cancer," said Aunt Bunny, "so they sewed him right back up again. The doctor told Minerva there was nothing anybody could do."

Pean's funeral was the first one I ever went to, and I was shocked by the sight of my first dead human body. It didn't look like Pean at all. It was shaved, there was no hat on its head, and it was laid out straight. It wasn't hunched over. A total stranger in Pean's casket.

Minerva put on a good show, weeping and wailing for days before, during, and long after the funeral.

"During the services she broke down four times," said Aunt Bunny. "It was so bad once that the minister had trouble finishing his prayer."

"It was just awful," my mother said.

"She's lived a hard life, and it's going to get harder now," Aunt Eller added.

Then there was the morning of Minerva's confession.

It happened about two months after Pean's death. I was sixteen and sleeping late on a Saturday morning. My bedroom was right over our kitchen so I could hear all the kitchen gossip through the floor register. I awoke that morning to Minerva's pounding on the front door and screaming for my mother.

"Minerva, what is it? What is it?" my mother was saying, trying to calm the hysterical woman down, but not having much luck.

"I've never had sexual intercourse!" she kept screaming over and over, sobbing in between exclamations.

"Well, ya didn't miss that much, Minerva," my mother said, but Minerva didn't seem to be much comforted by this. My mother has always hated such scenes of great hysteria. She likes things to be under tight control, and when she couldn't quiet Minerva down, she hollered for me. When I came into the kitchen, Minerva did stop her wailing. She put her head down on the table and quietly sobbed. After a while, my mother took her back across the road to her house, and then spent the rest of the day running around talking to all the neighbors on the phone, trying to get some kind of common consensus, especially among the relatives, over what was to be done.

Nothing was for a few weeks. We'd hear reports that Minerva was stealing from the stores in Ellsworth, that she had made a strange remark to someone in church, and that she had several long talks with the Baptist minister. One parishioner told the story that Minerva had asked the minister if a strict Baptist lady like her, at her age, could become a nun.

It was on Halloween night that fall, when Cousin Lillie and I were taking our younger cousins and neighbor kids from house to house trick-or-treating, that Lillie and I saw a sight we'll never forget. Some of the kids wanted to knock on Minerva's door because over the years she had always been very generous with us all on Halloween, giving us homemade fudge and apples. Because of what had been happening to Minerva, however, Lillie and I weren't sure that the kids should bother her. We told them to wait by the roadside while we went around to the back of the house where Minerva's bedroom was to see if she was still up. The front of the house was dark because the house was still divided and the front was Allard's and Myra's part. But the kitchen side window in Minerva's apartment, was dark, too. Lillie and I crept quietly around back, and there we saw her in the light of her bedroom window. She was naked and on the edge of her bed feeling her breasts and mumbling something about how she loved Jesus. Both of us wanted to laugh, but we were also scared, and we scurried back to the kids telling them that evidently Minerva could not be bothered tonight.

It wasn't too many weeks after that when one Sunday a neighbor man, who had been good enough to drive Minerva back and forth to church, came to see my parents. He told them how the church members felt that something had to be done right away about Minerva, how she was carrying on in church bothering the services and everybody with her crazy chattering and screaming. Evidently, instead of singing the hymns along with everyone else, she'd stand up and scream to the top of her lungs until the end of the music.

So Minerva had to leave her home. Allard and Myra were called, and they came down from Bangor to get her. And then came a period of Minerva's life when she had to be institutionalized from mental hospital to halfway house, and finally in her seventies in a nursing home.

Aunt Myra would come down on the weekends with Uncle Allard, and sometimes she would talk with my mother about Minerva.

"How is she?" my mother would ask.

"Oh, she's fat and healthy, happier than she's ever been," said Myra. "She goes to church all the time, and the only thing we've had trouble with is God's Gold Book Plan."

"What's that?"

"Oh, some crazy religious organization down south. We wondered what was happening to her Social Security check, since the nursing home called Allard and told him that Minerva hadn't paid for two months. It seems that she sent her whole check to this Reverend and God's Gold Book Plan. It's one of those crooked schemes that bilk poor crazy women like Minerva out of what little money they have. You send away for this little gold book that the minister has prayed over and you send him money every month for his prayers, and according to him you'll finally learn how to budget yourself and have more money. But it's him, of course, that gets the money. All you get is broke. Minerva didn't even have enough last week for her week's supply of Ben-Gay."

"What does she do with so much Ben-Gay?" my mother asked.

"Covers her whole body with it all the time. She stinks to the high heavens, so you can't sit in the same room with her for very long; but she claims she needs it every day to soothe her aches and pains."

I was listening in on this conversation, and as a teenager I had begun to be curious as to why some couples around town were couples. Some marriages didn't make much sense to me, especially if they were non-sexual and childless, so I asked Aunt Myra why Minerva married Pean in the first place.

She answered without hesitation. "Well, it seems to me Minerva needed a home, and Pean needed someone to take care of him. Simple as that."

My mother agreed, adding, "The problem was that Minerva needed taking care of, too. She was always great about starting all these plans, but she never knew how to end 'em."

YELLOW BIRCH TONIC

Rebecca Cummings

1910

It seemed to happen almost overnight. One day Matti had a full head of yellow-blond hair which he slicked back with water whenever he washed, and the next, his hair came out by the handful so that his scalp showed, shiny and bald. Matti was quick to blame Cousin Kenu's comb, which he had pocketed after the funeral for Erkki Seilonen's mother. He threw it away, but still his hair grew thinner.

More than once that winter, Kaisa walked into the kitchen to find her husband arranging what little hair he had so that it covered the receding hairline. The first time, Matti jumped aside and busied himself with brushing the dust from his shoulders. The second time, he complained about a bruise on his forehead, although Kaisa couldn't see a thing there. The third time, he opened his mouth to examine his molars.

"You fool!" she snapped. "Of course you're going bald. You're getting on in years, aren't you?"

The remark stung. He wasn't yet thirty.

Matti felt a pang of envy each time he saw a healthy head of hair. Sitting behind the Nurmi brothers in church, he saw that they had no less hair than they had ever had. And Sulo was three years older than Matti. Amos Cole, the proprietor of the Edom General Store, had a plenteous mass of wavy hair, snow-white though it was. And as Matti sat in Barker's Barber Shop with a hot towel over his face, he watched as a mound of curly hair piled up under John Thompson, the blacksmith.

It was towards the end of mud season, but still well before spring planting, when Matti hitched the horse to the express wagon so that he and Kaisa could go for a visit to Erkki Seilonen's. Kaisa, wanting to take some little gift, carried on her lap a glass jar of maple syrup, freshly made only three weeks earlier. After Matti and Kaisa had learned to tap the sugar maples that grew along their eastern boundary, they boiled the clear sap into dark sweet syrup each spring to spoon over breakfast porridge, hot biscuits and puffy oven-baked pancake.

"This syrup reminds me," Erkki said, eyeing the sparkling jar on the table, as his wife Mari and their robust daughter Este scurried to prepare the meal while talking with Kaisa, "that sap from a birch tree is supposed to cure baldness."

Although he pretended that it didn't matter to him, Matti's ears were open wide. After a little silence, he asked, "Fresh or boiled?" But then he said, as though more weighty matters occupied him, "If you don't have enough seed potatoes this year,

I've got some to sell."

"Fresh. Not boiled," Erkki said. "Rubbed onto the head before meals. Three times a day." Erkki reached into his pocket for a worn leather pouch and tapped stringy tobacco into a scrap of newspaper and then, licking it along the edge to seal it, added, "I've got more seed potatoes than I need. But you might want to see Viljo Heikkinen. I think his rotted in the cellar."

"We'll stop by on our way home. Uh — The sap of a birch? It runs late, doesn't it?"

"After the tree buds." The end of Erkki's cigarette flared as he lit it. "Yes. After the tree buds." He exhaled white smoke from his mouth and nostrils.

"Hmmm—" Matti said.

It was a morning bursting with promise of the season to come: the air fresh, the sky clear and blue. After having given the matter considerable thought, Matti chose his trees, two healthy yellow birch. Yellow birch rather than white or gray, yellow being the color that most nearly matched his hair.

Crossing the lower field which was wet and spongy from the steady rains of the days before, Matti carried a drill and two buckets, one clinking with the two spouts inside rolling back and forth. Muddy water gushed under his boots.

Clear sap spurted as soon as he pulled the drill bit from the hole. In excitement, Matti wet his hands under the steady run and rubbed the cool sap over his head. He was immediately disappointed that — other than the sticky wetness — he didn't feel a thing out of the ordinary. But of course it's too early, he told himself. This will take time. After all, a baby doesn't grow hair overnight. He set his buckets and hurried off, swatting at a swarm of pesky black flies.

It was nearly noon when Matti returned with two empty jugs and was amazed to see that the buckets were almost full. He poured the sap into jugs and hung the buckets back under the spouts. Again he wet his hands with the clear sap and slathered it onto his head. And again he fought off a cloud of biting black flies as he hurried home through the wet field.

The black flies chewed his arms and neck and head when he made his third trip, late that afternoon. Although the buckets were running over, Matti could see that the run was nearly spent. But with four full jugs, he had enough to grow more hair than he'd be able to handle. Unless he were willing to sit in Barker's barber chair once a week, his hair would probably be longer than any of the prophets. He could almost swear that this time he felt a little tingle to his scalp. Wouldn't Kaisa be surprised to see him with a full head of hair! *Old man*, she had started calling him. Why, he'd be looking five years younger before he knew it. Maybe even ten!

That evening while Kaisa was busy in the back room, Matti examined his milky scalp in the oak-framed mirror. Could it be that he saw a yellow-blond wisp or two more?

Sauna was a dilemma. He wasn't sure whether or not to wash his head. He certainly didn't want to tamper with the beneficial aspects of the yellow birch tonic, but he had always been particular about cleanliness. Even in his lumber camp days, when some of the men didn't wash for a whole season, Matti had been the one to insist on building a *sauna* and heating it at least once a week. So sitting on the low stool in *sauna*, he started to pour a bucket of water over his head but then stopped. Once he had hair, he decided, he'd wash it all he wanted. There would probably be so much that washing it would be a nuisance. But for now, he would scrub only to the hairline, leaving his scalp free to grow hair. Anxiously, he touched his fingertips to the top of his head, sticky from the steam and sweat.

For the next few weeks, Matti trekked to the cellar before each meal to rub a generous handful of yellow birch tonic onto his scaly scalp. Kaisa's lips tightened with each anointment. In the evenings she thumbed through the leather-bound Bible, seeking those verses that would speak to her husband.

"Ah-ha, old man!" she cried out, laying her knitting needles aside and running her finger along the lines as she read aloud from the book of Samuel. "I would say this is proof enough. It's perfectly clear that if Absalom hadn't been so vain as to let his hair grow long, he never would have gotten caught up in that oak tree while out riding. And then be fair game for his enemies, hanging by his hair. Here it is. The word of God. Right in the Holy Bible. Now throw that stuff away!"

"Throw it away? It's God's will that I ever learned to use it!"

"God's will?" She waved an empty knitting needle in his face. "Remember the Psalm? 'Who shall ascend unto the hill of the Lord...? He that hath clean hands...who hath not lifted up his soul unto vanity.'"

"But don't *you* remember that 'All is vanity...'?" Then he added, with a triumphant smirk, "'And VEXATION of the spirit'!"

In the last week of June, summer settled in with a fierce vengeance. Each morning, for days on end, the sun rose through a reddish glow, the air thick and heavy. Each afternoon, Kaisa watched as huge white thunderclouds mounted over the hills to the west. She waited for the crack that would break the spell, but the clouds drifted off. At night, Matti and Kaisa tossed on limp, damp sheets in the airless loft. Even though Kaisa had pulled back the flowered curtain that covered the doorway to the spare room and had opened the windows at each end, not a breeze stirred.

It was early one afternoon when Matti hung up his scythe and said that he was going into town. It was too hot to work. And besides, the hay chaff had stuffed his head. Then he sneezed, a wet, spattering sneeze.

Kaisa finished the ironing and swept the woodshed. She got the cows and did the evening chores. Since Matti still hadn't returned, she ate supper alone and went to bed.

Late though it was, Kaisa lay awake and heard the squeak of wagon wheels. She could tell from the way Matti stumbled as he climbed the stairs to the loft that he had stopped by Vaino Mustonen's to cool off on the way home. As soon as Matti touched the pillow, he began to snore. Kaisa slipped out of bed and tiptoed down the stairs to go outside and sit on the front stoop.

A whippoorwill shrilled its unbreaking call from beneath a shadowy apple tree on the far stone wall. Again and again. Does it ever stop? she wondered. Doesn't it stop to breathe? The night air was damp, the grass wonderfully dewy under her bare feet. She closed her eyes, leaning her head against the rough wood of the door frame.

In her tiredness, she thought about the child, a son, delivered in its fifth month last winter. She relived the sorrow. Were she and Matti never to be blessed with children? A farm without children?

The whippoorwill stopped.

She almost dozed. And then from across the field, its faint cry started again. *Whip-poor-will. Whip-poor-will.*

The sun the next morning was hot and red. At breakfast, Kaisa was already sticky from the heat. When Matti complained that the bread was stale, she snapped, "Maybe you'd better learn to bake your own bread! I'd say it's good enough for someone who doesn't know to come home at night."

She sat at the table and spooned listlessly at her gummy rice porridge. There was a fetid smell in the kitchen, and she got up to sniff at the drain in the black slate sink. But the problem didn't seem to be there. The motionless air in the close room and the rank odor were so overpowering that she took her bowl outside and sat on the still shaded front stoop.

While Matti drove the brown horse in front of the hay rake, Kaisa pulled the cumbersome bull rake along the edges of the field. Hay was too valuable to lose even a trace. She paused in the shade of a spreading apple tree. It wasn't even mid-morning, and already it felt like mid-afternoon. She shoved her wet, stringy hair, falling out of its bun, away from her face. She had never known such heat. It had never been so hot back in Finland.

She watched through weary eyes as Matti, on the far side of the shimmering field, kept an eye on the mounding windrow behind him as the horse made the turn towards where she stood. Matti twisted in a sneeze. And then again. She waited for another. There. He pulled his handkerchief from his pocket, flicking it like a banner, and wiped it over his face. The horse, its head low, continued plodding towards her, over the buzzing field of freshly cut hay spotted with fading daisy and drying purple vetch. She could smell the heat of the horse as it drew closer.

"I forgot to tell you," Matti called down to her from his perch on the iron seat of the hay rake, "that I saw Pastori Halme in town yesterday. I told him to come and eat with us today." He took off his hat and rubbed his arm over his glistening head.

"What? To do what?" For a second, Kaisa thought that Matti had said that Pastori Halme was coming to eat. The heat seemed to be affecting her.

"There's no need to make a fuss," he said, climbing down from the rake. "Just what we always have." He went for the water jug, nestled amongst the weeds at the base of the tree. His shirt stuck wetly to his back. He pushed at his straw hat with his thumb and tipped the jug to drink. Water ran down his chin and neck. Catching the dribbling water on the back of his hand, he said, "And he's bringing the visiting pastor." He held the jug out for Kaisa.

"What? What are you talking about, old man? What visiting pastor?" Kaisa eyed her red-faced husband in annoyance. His nose was peeling, and the birch sap looked slimy along the edge of his hat. She ran her dry tongue over her lips, but she didn't reach for the jug.

"Pastori Salminen! Have you forgotten? From the synod. He's come for the annual meeting and the picnic on Sunday. I told them to come here for dinner today."

"PASTORI SALMINEN?"

"I told you. I saw them in town —"

But Kaisa had already dropped the bull rake and had started for the house.

Now what? Her mind raced, even as she slid over the slippery hay. A visiting pastor? For dinner? What could she possibly do so late in the morning? She had been planning on fried pork rind and potatoes. But for a visiting pastor? She held her skirt high, so that her black stockings showed to her knees, and leaped over the rows of raked hay. She couldn't give fried pork rind to a visiting pastor. But what else was there? She turned the corner of the barnyard, past the little henhouse. A hen? But there wasn't time.

The screen door to the kitchen clattered behind her as she hurried through with an armload of wood to feed the dying embers. In the rising heat, she peeled potatoes and threw them into a kettle to boil and then thought to also boil a half-dozen eggs. Scurrying to the garden, she grabbed for a huge handful of tender beet greens.

As the pots bubbled on the stove, she carried a pitcher of tepid water up the stairs to the stuffy bedroom beneath the eaves. She tore off her work clothes and, clad only in her modest undergarments, splashed water from the porcelain bowl onto her face and along her forearms. She quickly dried with the linen towel that hung over the harp and went to the mirror to pull her light brown hair back into a tidy bun, pinning it tightly with two wide-toothed combs. She slipped into her long-sleeved dark blue Sunday dress and arranged the white crocheted collar. With a final pat to her hair, she scooted down the stairs.

In the kitchen, she whisked her best lace cloth onto the wobbly table. She pulled one of the straight-backed chairs into the pantry so that she could stand on it to reach her company dishes, eggshell-colored with tiny roses around the rims, all stacked on the top shelf of the cupboard.

She anticipated the thick, heady odor of cream and the still, cool darkness of the milkhouse as she turned the handle of the door. Standing in the shaft of light, she blinked away the dimness. How pleasant to sit on a sawdust-covered chunk of ice and idle away the afternoon. The thought flirted with her imagination for only an instant. Instead, she reached for a star-stamped block of her own sweet butter and dipped fresh, cold milk from a wide-mouthed can into a glass pitcher.

She sliced the hard-boiled eggs into a milky gravy and spooned it over crisp pieces of pork rind. She cut thick slabs of rye bread and dished out the steaming potatoes and beet greens.

As she carried a deep, cut glass bowl of ruby-red strawberries swimming in sweet juice to the table, Matti flew past her through the kitchen and down the cellar steps. And as she put down the dessert saucers, he raced back to go upstairs and come down again in his brown wool suit. The screen door banged behind him as he hurried out to sit in the speckled shade of the towering maple tree in front of the house with Pastori Halme and the visiting Pastori Salminen. Kaisa's nose twitched. That odor again. Where was it coming from? She heard Matti sneeze. Once. Twice. And then the murmur of voices.

Everything was ready. The table set. The food on. She went to the window, standing just behind the gauzy curtain. Even in this heat, the visiting pastor's suit was stiff and prim, the white collar tight. She had been so busy she had forgotten how hot it was. She daubed at her face and neck with the hem of her long apron. And tired. She had never felt so tired. She thought about the cool, dark milkhouse with its smell of cream. How wonderful to go in and not come out at all. Instead, she went to the door to call the two pastors and her husband in to eat.

"...and for this food set before us, we thank Thee, O Lord," Pastori Salminen prayed, his voice as reedy as he was.

"Amen," they said, the men sitting at the table, Kaisa standing by the stove.

The two men of the church and Matti helped themselves to the meal Kaisa had so hastily prepared. Pastori Halme and Matti heaped their plates with potatoes and greens, smothering them with pork rind and gravy. Pastori Salminen, however, took only a spoonful of this and a bit of that.

A sluggish breeze wafted through the kitchen. That smell again! What was it? Kaisa sidled to the sink and sniffed. It was no more the drain than it had been earlier. She looked around.

"Have more?" Matti offered.

"Thank you, but no."

Silverware chinked against the plates.

A fly buzzed over Matti's crusted head. He shooed it away, his arm stiff in the tight suit.

"How long will you stay in Edom?" Matti's voice was thick and nasal. He snuffled.

"Until Monday. Then Portland. I have relatives —" Pastori Salminen eyed the buzzing fly.

Kaisa watched him watching the fly. Again she caught the smell.

"The haying?" Pastori Halme asked. He was shabby and faded beside Pastori Salminen. Something should be done. Some sewing. She'd talk to the women.

Matti mentioned the heat.

The walls pressed inward. Kaisa tugged with one finger at the scratchy crocheted collar. How could those men of the clergy wear such tight collars?

The fly perched on Matti's shoulder. If she could only grab for a newspaper from the corner cupboard. But not with company. Not with Pastori Salminen. Matti shrugged it off while shoveling another dripping knifeful of potato and gravy.

Pastori Salminen picked at the greens with his fork. "Your head? A disease?" he asked.

"Ah, it's —" Matti faltered. He was half-standing, stretching across the table, reaching for more of the gravied pork rind.

But Kaisa was there before her husband could touch the serving dish, shoving it at the visiting pastor.

It was then that she knew.

And so did Pastori Salminen, for she saw in horror that he took a starched white handkerchief from his breast pocket and held the folded cloth to his mouth and nose.

It was Matti! Her own husband. The yellow birch sap had gone rancid. And with his hay fever, he couldn't smell a thing. The fool!

She grasped the serving dish, refusing to give it up to him. Spots of heat enflamed her cheeks. "Have more!" she demanded of the visiting pastor.

Pastori Salminen dropped his handkerchief, looked to her flustered face and dipped out a scant spoonful of pork rind and gravy.

"More!"

Pastori Salminen drizzled a stream of gravy along the lace tablecloth.

"What's that?" Pastori Halme grunted, scraping his plate clean with a thick crust of rye bread.

Matti had loosened his shirt collar even before Pastori Halme's little black buggy had left the dooryard. He lost no time in getting upstairs to change back into his work clothes and stretching out in the thin grass under the maple tree, to let his meal digest.

Kaisa, listening to her husband's snores, at last sat down to eat. What a dunderhead Matti was, she thought. As though birch sap could grow hair. As though he needed hair to be a man! When she finished her meal, she resolved, she would take this matter into her own hands.

Leaving her dirty dishes on the table, she slipped down the stairs into the dank cellar. One and a quarter jugs of the putrid sap left. Lugging the slippery jugs back up into the bright kitchen, she poured the cloudy liquid down the drain, following it with a bucket of hot water and lye.

She was standing on a chair, putting the last rose-rimmed plate back on the top shelf of the pantry cupboard when Matti, his eyes heavy and the side of his face red and creased with the imprint of grass and leaves, came into the kitchen.

"There's no need for you to go down cellar for more of that sap," she said, not looking at him as she got down from the chair. She closed her nose to the rancid smell.

"Why not? What are you talking about?"

"Couldn't you tell? It spoiled. It smelled worse than pig swill. I threw it out. Down the drain." She shoved the chair back to the table.

"Can't a man have a thing in his own house?" Although Matti blustered, he had been beset lately with doubts about the efficacy of yellow birch tonic. But he felt it necessary to add, "It's working. I can feel it."

"All you feel are the flies biting your head!" However, then her voice sweetened and she said, "A man as young as you doesn't need to worry that losing a few hairs will make him an old grandfather. Why look at all you do. Enough for two men. Two *young* men."

Matti shrugged, annoyed. But he said, "Two?"

"We don't have a hired hand, do we? A hot day like this — Why don't you go out to the pump and wash your head. Think how refreshing it will feel."

"Well —" he said, scratching his head, smearing the sweaty sap. "Only because it's such a hot day." He started out but paused, holding the screen door open. "That Absalom must have looked pretty strange with so much hair. What do you think?"

Kaisa folded her large linen dish towel, embroidered along one edge with purple violets and tiny green vines, and hung it over the rack to dry. Cocking her head, she listened for the noisy squeak of the pump outside.

As though blown by the push of the pump handle, the curtains ruffled, and a sweet breeze floated through the room like a soft whisper. Kaisa sniffed. Rain. She went to the window.

Mountainous gray-bottomed clouds swelled in a murky sky over the western hills. The undersides of the leaves of the maple tree flashed silver as they whipped skyward.

"Matti!" she called, rushing outside. "Look!"

But Matti, his wet hair slicked over the receding hairline, was already harnessing the horse to the hay wagon. Hearing a far-off rumble of thunder, Kaisa grabbed for a pitchfork and hurried to meet him, out in the hayfield.

MOTES OF GRACE

S.T. Colby

Muriel was kind of a stringy thing. No meat on her, no color. She wore her hair pulled back in an elastic at the base of her neck and her skin had a waxy, sallow look, like it never saw the light. When Chester found her she was living on a closed-off ramp of the Mystic River Bridge, selling $2 tricks and boosting food from the PicPac on Boylston Street. Chester had just finished his correspondence courses. He was fully accredited as a preacher for the Church of God's Sinners and was working nights as a maintenance man at the YWCA. It was a little more than six months before they noticed he was peeking into the women's locker room through the ventilating grate that opened to the attic. The Board of Directors wouldn't even give him a hearing, but that was all right. God had found him early and crawled right inside, Chester knew for sure. The Voices had always come to him, directing him through this sin-filled world. The Board was but an instrument, steering Chester from the Sodom that was Boston. Muriel was the problem.

Chester had brought her along back to Trenton, Maine, and set up his Mission in the trailer Grams had left him. He held services every Saturday night and all day Sunday, and on Wednesday nights he held an informal group prayer meeting. Muriel served tea or kool-aid and brownies or peanut butter cookies to the group prayer meeting. She passed things around just right, okay, but she never "amen"-ed or "hallalujah"-ed when everyone else did. It was like she just watched, with this little smile on her face. "Her shit eating grin," Chester called it. Just watching and smiling and passing, and never a word for praise or prayer.

There were six of them, sometimes seven, who came regular on Wednesdays. If Ted McDonald wasn't quite sober but not yet really drunk by 6:30, he'd join his sister, Etta, in the straight-back chairs either side of the trailer door. Chester always had to concentrate especially hard on the Wednesday lessons because Etta's chair was directly across from his lectern and Chester could see right up her floral print cotton dress, past her stocking rolled on elastics to just above her knees, to the fact that she wore no underpants. Chester's mind would fill with Grams; how her big soft breasts had wrapped around him every night until he was eleven. "Good boy, Chester. Grams' best boy, you are," she'd said. And then she'd died, just like that, leaving Chester with only the smell of her Vicks and her peachblossom breath. The undertaker had had to pull him away from her that night and it had taken four big men to carry her body to the hearse. Etta was a lot like Grams, Chester thought. One of those heart-of-gold people, always doing for others. When Ted drank too much, always when there was no work for his skidder, she undressed him and got him safely to bed. She took rhubarb roots to the family homesteading on the Parkin's place — just walked right up there and introduced herself, important as anything. And she'd been the first to come to Chester's trailer Mission, bringing a raspberry pie welcome before he'd even got the cross out. "No. Nothing stringy about Etta." And Chester always prayed extra loud on Wednesdays, getting up a full head of steam and making it the best meeting of the week.

Chester was real proud of his Mission; starting with nothing but his diploma, the trailer and a two-and-a-half-foot-high electrified white plastic cross, he'd established a nice little following. The Saturday and Sunday collections and proceeds from craft sales brought in as much as $75 a week. What with food stamps and fuel assistance, Muriel had $624 in the shoe box under the bed. There were often as many as twenty-five people at Saturday services and thirty-five to forty every Sunday. Wednesday's prayer group was the core: Etta, Griffin, and Beatrice and George Moran, "real movers for the Voice," as Chester called them.

The Morans were always on hand. Beatrice knitted mittens during the meetings and made dozens of toilet-paper-roll covers, all to sell for the benefit of the Mission treasury. She bought naked plastic dolls at the Newberry's in Ellsworth and crocheted gowns and hats in variegated yarns. Each doll's legs slid neatly into the cardboard roll so the doll appeared to dance across the tank top or on the edge of the tub, skirt flounced out. George took the dolls to every summer craft show and the tourists scooped them up. The $78 for Chester's lectern — white pine, varnished to a high glossy finish with 'The Prophet' carved on the front — came entirely from the sale of toilet-paper-roll dolls. Chester had designated George as Mission Sexton because he owned a pickup truck.

Besides, after he put tarred paper around the foundation of the trailer and replaced the window in the rear door when Ted McDonald put his fist through it, it seemed the only thing to do.

Griffin came on Wednesdays with her boys. Griffin's boys couldn't sit still for Saturday or Sunday services and Griffin had learned never to leave them. A visiting nurse took her once for 45 minutes to the mobile health clinic to have an abscessed tooth pulled. Griffin explained carefully that she'd be right back but the twins set fire to the privy and trashed the garden all the same. "Scared," they said. But they couldn't explain further. Their behavior was model as long as Griffin was around; they never spoke out of turn and always said, "Yes, sir — No ma'am" in unison. Big boys for sixteen, "my Goliaths" she called them, they'd stand to either side of her when she offered up the three hymns she was sure of on her accordian, both singing in strong baritones.

Griffin had never sent the boys to school after that first day. They had just turned six and had left on the bus in the matching sweaters Griffin had made herself, carrying paper sacks filled with thick slices of butter-and-jam-slathered bread. She had had great expectations. School would transform all their lives somehow. The boys would open up to the world and magically take themselves and her away from Trenton to a life somewhere else. Life would be for them like she saw pictured in the Sears catalogue pages, full of pretty things. Sheer curtains, a matching parlor set with wooden arms, and scattter rugs in the bedroom. Except the boys were afraid of all the strangeness and they cried and wet their pants and the principal brought them home by 10:15, saying they might be ready next year. And when next year came, Griffin couldn't bear to be apart from them. Once the State sent a letter saying they'd have to go, they even sent a man to fetch them. But the boys ran off and hid in the woods. Griffin flatly told the State man they'd up and run off, and no one ever bothered again. So Griffin gave them all she knew. They had manners and they split wood, they foraged and they loved, and every Wednesday they went to the group prayer meeting. Griffin put aside her expectations and the boys had none, so it seemed enough for the three of them.

Once Chester got a thing in his mind he'd worry it, "hang on to the throat of it like a pit bull," Grams always said, until it was done with. Like the sled. His seventh winter had sent snows perfect for sliding, all the neighborhood out past daylight, ears burning, bladders teased to bursting by the cold for the joy of one more run down Titcomb's Hill. Grams made Chester a sled from a Western Auto carton she'd found on the dump. It worked fair enough but Chester wanted a real sled. He could taste the excitement of the idea, rising up like gall in his mouth. At night he'd dream on it so clear he'd wake up knowing it was leaning against the woodpile. It was red with a golden eagle on the bellywhomp part, "Shiny runners — faster than silverfish, Grams." Rodney Spear had just such a sled. Snub-nosed-with-a-special-pair-of-sneakers-just-for-playing-basketball-Rodney had Chester's sled. He brought it to Titcomb's Hill Christmas night and wouldn't let anybody try a turn on it. "Don't you put your dirty hands on my sled, neither, Chester." Christmas night, 1954, and seven-year-old Chester snuck around the edge of the lake from Rodney Spear's house, carrying the sled all the way so no track marks showed. He used a long branch to push it out onto the thin ice of the spring hole and just kept throwing boulders from the retaining wall at it until it broke through. It hurt him to see it disappear like that. First the front sort of cracked into the ice and it hung there through three more rocks, to just slip away then, quiet. But he felt better when it was done with. No more "realer than real" dreams. And the Voices, sometimes so loud they would drive him to yell out, "Stop!" quieted too. Until that State woman tried to take him away from Grams.

That had been quite a business. The fall she'd come by the farm, Chester was nine and a half. The school had called on her after Chester confessed to strangling all his teacher's chickens and had refused to apologize in any way at all. He knew he'd been right to do it. Why, Chester'd even warned Mr. Poulin of dire happenings if he didn't keep his hands to himself, but Mr. Poulin would insist, keeping Chester after to clap erasers and touching and poking in ways Chester didn't like. Grams never asked any questions after he explained it was a Voice-directed thing, and right to do. She even told the school that Chester would never do a thing he didn't know to be right and that he was real good, her "best boy," but that State woman came all the same. She came all decked out in a ruffled blouse and wouldn't have a piece of Gram's chocolate mayonnaise cake — made special — or even a cup of tea. Chester hid in the kitchen woodbox and listened while she and Grams talked. After she left, Grams told him the woman would be back on Wednesday next to take him to live with some people in Bangor and there was nothing to be done for it. Chester thought on the problem quite a bit. Couldn't sleep or even eat, the dreams and messages coming in the morning, all the time, suggesting one solution, then another. Late Tuesday night he took the biggest wrench he could find to the bridge over Parker's Gorge and loosened the bolts in every strut. It was a pretty hard job. The wrench was heavy and the bolts were rusty and hard to move. Chester nearly fell a time or two. Chester slept like a turnip Tuesday night, though, knowing the Voices had shown the way. No one came up the town road unless they were coming to Grams.

The highway department said they didn't understand why the bridge hadn't given way years ago, having been built for buggies, and it was the town's responsibility anyway. The Selectmen said it was a private-way owned by the railroad who said, "Prove it." The State woman's family tried to sue everybody, but it all simmered down after a while.

Now Muriel was in his mind, bothering his sleep somehow, all mixed in with his calling and Boylston Street, and stuff long done with. All kind of mixed together and keeping him from concentrating on his Mission.

Chester couldn't remember right when things started changing. One day Griffin contradicted him when he gave his meaning to the lesson — the one about rendering unto Caesar and unto God what was due on either count — how supporting his Mission and his work would take care of the whole kit and kaboodle, Chester sort of being God's business manager and Caesar's tax man all rolled into one. Griffin was nice enough about it, saying her coming every Wednesday to the Mission didn't seem to stop Caesar from cutting her food stamp allotment when she'd sold off the standing timber along the brook and got $4,000 for it, most of which she gave to the Mission. He felt the perfect fool when everybody laughed. Then they laughed again when Muriel said there might be ways around God, but Caesar would get you in the end for sure.

He stayed up half the night on that one, not getting to sleep until he'd settled a black eye on Muriel for making jokes about such important matters. Next thing, Ted McDonald was transplanting geraniums around the cross by the trailer steps. When Chester questioned him about it he said Muriel had asked him to. Finally, on her seventeenth birthday, Muriel just went right out and got her hair cut and made curly all over her head, little soft ringlets. Griffin said, "She looks just like a young Jesus, don't she Chester: you know, in that picture when he was twelve or so, preaching in the yard of that big Jew church." And she showed him the picture. Chester had to agree, but it really irked him, Muriel going out and doing it without even asking and then Griffin thinking it was fine. Muriel just smiled and kept her eyes down like Chester'd taught her a good woman should. "Like butter wouldn't melt in her mouth and her shit don't stink," Chester thought. And George started taking her for rides in his pickup. "Want to ride along with Bea's mittens to the Congregational Bazaar? We'll stop on the way back, at that soft ice-cream place in Veazie. How'd ya like a trip to the lumber yard, Muriel?" Worse yet, Etta changed her accustomed Wednesday seat, making it a point to be by Muriel and hopping up to help pass cookies and kool-aid around. She even made brownies and brought them one week, "so Muriel can spend time on more important matters," she said.

It had taken a lot of patience but Chester felt he'd got Muriel nearly straightened out from the Boston days. He'd housed her and fed her and "gotten the wildness out of her," the wild streak taking some strictness, at first, to tame. For a month she'd walked around with what looked to be permanent indentations in her knees, her penance for numerous transgressions to spend long hours kneeling on a thick layer of dried peas spread in the bottom of the shower stall. But she'd been saved, in spite of herself. She kept the trailer clean and always had Chester's dinner ready at exactly 4:30 every afternoon. No doubt she was stringy, but she provided a man enough of what's needed to keep him from meanness, "without any sass, too." And now, after two pretty good years and the Mission really getting going, something was festering. He couldn't put his finger on it yet, but it was there, brewing up.

For one thing, Chester was dreaming again. At first, vague, grey tossings, lately turned to recurring, insistent images. Being swallowed whole like Jonah. Being invisible, disappeared somehow, but still there, with things going on around him as though nothing had changed. And for a whole week he took to waking up at exactly 2:30 every morning in a cold sweat. He had actually had to will himself to stay in his bed after the first three nights. The dream had been so real that he hadn't been able to resist walking out to the kitchen in his bare feet to make certain it wasn't really going on: Mr. Poulin and that State woman were sitting in the little dining nook, laughing up a storm and drinking cider from the green thumbprint glasses Muriel'd won in the penny toss at the Bangor Fair. Then, one morning while he was shaving, Muriel's face appeared in the mirror, startling him so he cut himself. "I must'a been walking by, Chester." But she was way in the other end of the trailer and he had had to go all the way up the hallway and across the kitchen to slap her. "Look here. You've left your good glasses out, too. Damn slut." And he'd slapped her again.

The situation certainly required some action. But the trusted messages, the Voices, wouldn't come, and Chester knew he'd have to wait, like always, for the way to be revealed. Meantimes, his head ached for lack of sleep and from chewing on the matter so.

Etta and Griffin both said how peaked he looked. Muriel took to bringing him a cup of bouillon around 2 o'clock every afternoon, cajoling him into drinking it all down, "for your own good, Chester. For the Mission, then. Come on now."

Saturday afternoon Chester felt especially riled up about how things weren't going his way. He just dropped everything, and went over to Beatrice's and George's place with a *Family Circle* "how to" page for birdhouses he thought George could make in quantity for craft sales. George was in the workshop and, though he said how glad he was to see Chester and how he sure could do those birdhouses, easy as anything, Chester didn't like the feel of things at all. "Not like you, Chester, to come around on a Saturday," George said. He was building something like a dock or a mudwalk, "a secret, a surprise. A little something Muriel has me working on." And he changed the subject back to birdhouses, suggesting yellow paint with blue trim and a couple of finishing details not shown on the plans. "Little shutters, I think. In blue. Be real cute, Chester." Beatrice brought out some lemonade and observed that Chester looked a little pale. "You know, you've not looked well all summer, Chester. And coming by on a Saturday, that's not like you. Muriel says you're hardly sleeping nights, up roaming the trailer, muttering and pacing about. It won't do the sheep no good if the wolf gets the shepherd, ya know." And she hurried back to the house, "all a'bustle," Chester thought, "and humming."

George invited Chester around back to see how well his new asparagus bed had taken, despite the summer having been so dry.

Just standing there in the sun, listening to George, Chester knew everything should be fine. Really. These were his people and he hadn't been himself lately. Here, with a head full of katydids in bright, three o'clock sun, all should be well: just listening to George; just sipping lemonade; just staring beyond the edge of the garden, into the full ripe hay, shimmering and bobbing like a great beige sea; there was Grams, waist-high in the hay, soft and smiling like he was eleven again. The hair rose on the back of his neck and the chill of gooseflesh pulled him tight into himself. So tight, he thought his head might burst, and he fell over into the asparagus, mouth gaping, eyes fixed on Grams. He heard George call for Beatrice, who came out "all a'bustle."

"Muriel said it was coming, just this way. She said, 'Mark me, friends. He'll fall over, right to the ground, one day. And we'll have to be ready.' Are we ready, George?"

"It's done."

Chester could see Grams, still smiling in the hay, all the while they fetched the wheelchair and lifted him in. "My good boy," she seemed to say. "Best boy" Beatrice tucked the afghan around his legs, "made specially for this, Chester. Griffin worked every spare minute to have it ready for you." It was white with yellow roses twining around a large red cross. "And Beatrice did the lettering, Chester. She's working the same thing in potholders, to sell," George pridefully pointing to 'Chester, First Prophet' worked in dark blue yarn, cross-stitched, and landing about his knees. "Smaller, of course, in the potholders."

George went off somewhere but everyone else seemed to be trampling about the asparagus suddenly, Etta crying and alternately hugging Ted, then Griffin's boys, saying how exciting, to be witness to a real prophecy, to know two real prophets.

Then Muriel was there, looking not in the least stringy. She was wearing a white dress with blue trim on the pocket, and as she came close to Chester's wheelchair he saw, 'Second Prophet' cross-stitched there. "Like Chester always said, even way back in Boston," she said. "Open yourself to the Voice and it will direct you." And she kept her eyes cast down just right, and she had the sweetest smile.

Chester's mouth kept opening and sort of closing back up, but no sounds came out, only a little spittle. Griffin kept wiping his chin with a kleenex.

Chester lost sight of Grams as Muriel wheeled the chair across the yard. George had opened the tailgate on the pickup and put a ramp up so Muriel pushed Chester right up into the back end with no trouble at all. "Pretty slick, Muriel," George said. "Fits right up to the trailer door, too. Measured it out real careful, you did. Beatrice and Etta in front with me. Muriel, you can sit on Etta's lap. Ted and the boys in back."

"You boys see that chair don't roll around none," Muriel said. And George closed the tailgate real gentle.

"We'll be all settled in at the trailer in plenty of time for Saturday service," Etta said. "And I'm so proud, Muriel. Ted cut the lectern down, right on the line you drew. Sits level as can be."

Chester's mouth kept opening and closing and Griffin handed the kleenex to Ted.

GETTING DRUNK WITH MY FATHER
Stephen Petroff

I wish I was sitting on a porch in Hell drinking whiskey
as I was the night my father & I got drunk.
This was the night I asked him about the stones that rise
out of the ground in the Spring, and he told me they'll
never stop coming up into the air because they want to
feel the warm hands that toss them out of gardens

> *Those stones* (he said) *don't come from*
> *Hell — they're in the dirt under the*
> *ground, they're innocent*
> *Until we touch 'em.*

This was also the night I decided to tell him about the
well where I get all the deep cold water.
So that night in bottles of deep cold bourbon I shouted
The Northerners have arrived from the South!
With this statement I established my position
and I felt I had never before been so well understood.

And as never before it was possible to exchange and list
our Inventory of Pains and Catalog of Ships.

> *Those fieldstones long outlast us*
> (he said) *but as soon as we touch them*
> *they're on their way offstage.*
> *It's called Contamination.*

I think of the brief lives of stones when I hear
the thousand-year winds in my daughter's breath.

> *Children can't be monuments*
> *but everyone keeps trying*

The best part of child-raising is what I do in my sleep —
all I can offer is what happens at Night.

> *I don't know if any of us*
> *are fit to raise children*

Living in town I realized I'm the last one to put on my winter
coat & the last to take it off. I don't think of my children
as a sort of handsome gravestone, but I count on them
to save me.

> *Can you be saved by stones*
> *rattling around on a beach?*

I sure hope so! I've bet everything I have on it.
But these mugs aren't filled with accusing spirits.

> *No, these are not*
> *accusing spirits*
> *and we've never talked*
> *like this before.*

Well — the first time my daughter kissed me there was a
screendoor between us — that's true —
No symbolism there —

And whether it's family or friends
Few people like to smell stale sweat because fresh sweat
is so alive it stills any wish for lesser experiences.

> *But how do you keep the sweat fresh?*

That's right! The lack of fresh sweat
leads off the Inventory of Pains.
At the end of most days my friends lie slain.

> *You kill them off when they can't do the*
> *Impossible — you should only see them*
> *once a year*

As it IS I only see them once a year

> *You should only see them once in a*
> *lifetime — love can look so hideous*

All this time I thought I lived in Heaven while I walked in a
landscape
of men & women mute
and trees calling like children.

> *The trouble with this Universe is,*
> *it's too easy to get used to it —*
> *You start thinking,*
> *Hell isn't such a bad place,*
> *if you can just get at the thermostat.*

Love is hideous? Hell *is* Heavenly.
There are islands, right now, where babies are born.
Twice, I've seen it happen.

> *It's nothing watching a baby being born.*
> *Suppose we were drunk with God —*
> *Now think about the birth of Jehovah.*
> *It'd make you puke to watch it.*

He never was a boy.
He was always FULL-grown.
Think about that.
Don't we have some maps of the moon
around here?

I would have to begin my Inventory of Gods with a
declaration to all: the only reason behind my art is
to put the cards on the table. I never talk about another
world, not yet, an Inventory of Gods includes an
Inventory of Birds — and permit me, I see demons —

Anyone who doesn't believe in demons
has his eyes closed — There may not be
one in every town, but sometimes you
might run into a whole platoon of demons.

I've counted tusked gods among the mleccha yavanas
beheaded gods rolling at the shoreline, & drunken gods

I've heard them fools talking when
they didn't think I was listening —
"Boy wait'll I catch that son of a bitch
in town" — that was always the big
thing —
"If I ever catch him in town —"
But I'd go off-base into a bar, &
they'd be all smiles — "Sarge!
Let me buy you a drink, Sarge!
Let me buy you a drink!"
Buy me a drink? You can
buy me a drink. *Goddamn RIGHT!*
That's from the Inventory of Men &

one hundred out of one hundred
paint the skirt around their trailers
once a year & call it good.
That's how they ended up, without
even a shack in the woods where
they can go drink a quart of whiskey
once in a while.

So my list includes an ugly god & a charismatic god.

You want to know about charisma?
When I was dead drunk I've had
men who hated my guts spread a
blanket over me so I wouldn't
freeze to death.

I've listed the baby god I've seen myself
and the old goat-god I've been told about.

You might as well believe those stories.
These whizz-kids think it's great they have
these computers that never make a mistake
but think of how many times in your life
you haven't been able to
figure something out
& then had some stupid fellow give you the
answer. Sometimes it takes a stupid man
to see something from the right angle.

I was standing painting in a field one day staring straight
ahead with the sun beside me when something
touched my shoulder.
It was so light & strange like electricity without a sting,
my first thought was, "An Angel has landed on my shoulder!"

I turned my head to look into his face, & it was a chickadee,
that flew away —

> But you still think it was an angel
> more or less

More than ever I'm convinced —
the way it felt with its claw hooked in my shirt —

> We had a Studebaker when you was born
> — that was a good car, it never
> overheated more than 50 yards from
> a river

Now that would be my idea of a Visionary Car.

> There's an old saying,
> "Many a Myshkin
> Makes a Munchkin"

No No The old saying is,
"Blessings old man for crossing the road."

> What does that mean?

I don't know.

> Now I understand.
> But any old man I ever knew
> more often than not
> they toppled his statues
> & gouged out the eyes.

Well, I've taken it upon myself to offer blessings.
That's my next act.
First, the cards on the table
Then blessings for all, my treat.

> It sounds like the Insanity Defense.
> People won't put up with it anymore —

not that they ever did.

I've been trying to make art for 15 years. People who
never spent 10 minutes out of their lives thinking about
art have no business lecturing me. At least I offer them
kisses through a screendoor, the same as I do my family.

> *Be careful, you'll be like my mother*
> *before she went into the hospital.*
> *She saw things no one else could see*
> *and they just terrified her.*

At the same time it has taken me quite a few years to
begin to admit that I see things & hear voices.
So far they have never terrified me.

> *Usually if you don't let those things*
> *bother you, & just get a good night's*
> *sleep, they'll work themselves out.*

These aren't fearsome voices, or accusing spirits.
My daughter said, "Daddy, stop talking like a demon,"
and I took her literally.

> *Like a rehabilitated mental patient.*
> *But every once in a while one of them*
> *will put a gun behind the doctor's ear*
> *& say "Ooh, how does this feel?*
> *Is it cold?"*

Well, I'm not offended by the comparison — because
there is such a Strange Beauty in Paranoia. It vibrates
before the eye like velvet. It tastes like mayonnaise-jar-
booze. I almost see myself on a warm day in December
walking across a park, windy morning, drinking from the
mayonnaise jar.

It's as fun as being lost in the woods.

> *Moss is in sympathy with those*
> *who are lost in the woods.*

What about ferns?

> *Ferns see no reason why*
> *you shouldn't stay lost.*

I think I will be lost until I see the Triumph of the Heart
over its tools.

> *This is something we can't do in*
> *the outside world anymore —*
> *It's too bad, I'd like to see it*
> *myself — Don't we have some*
> *maps of the Moon around here?*

I just want some of your sage advice.

> *I can give you some sage advice.*
> *Can you remember anything you*
> *ever learned from me?*

3 Things: Measure twice & saw once.

Load light & go often.

& Never cut towards yourself.

That last one's the only one I don't follow.

> *Well, there's no reason why*
> *you shouldn't cut towards yourself,*
> *but I still say it's good advice*
> *to give a kid.*
> *Because you know what can happen*
> *if he tears himself up.*

Yes, & I've seen it: the chairs at the edge of the
room are alive, the walls are alive, the window & windowpanes

are alive, the casket of glowing wood is alive, but the body in
the casket is not alive — you can clearly see: The Soul Has Fled.
You see the sunlight all around the husk. And time rolls by,
the trees extend & dance right where they stand,
birds swing across the sky east to west,
but time is dead & there are no minutes
inside the husk. Everyone in the room is thinking,
"This garment was so seamless. What *on earth* could have torn it?"

> *Well, my secret is:*
> *I don't give a Goddamn*
> *whether I die or not.*

he spoke this line with a voice like the stones that come to the
surface of the earth,
lifted his hand, palm out, in the gesture that means
No Fear.

> *I got together last year with my old*
> *First Sgt., and I said, "We had some*
> *good times, didn't we?"*
> *And he said, "But you was always*
> *so bad — you always used to tear*
> *the sink out of the wall &*
> *throw it through the barracks window —"*
> *But that's the way it is —*
> *once you tear the sink out of the wall*
> *& throw it through the window,*
> *from then on, everytime someone*
> *tears the sink out of the wall*
> *& throws it through the window,*
> *they think you did it.*

SMOKE

Lucy Honig

Labor Day had been a scorcher and the day after was starting hot too. But there was a considerable amount of smoke coming out of Cecil White's chimney.

A Volkswagen van from Massachusetts went by, already lost on its way from the lake, and didn't notice. When the road fizzled out and the van circled back it still didn't notice. Twenty minutes later a Winnebago from New Jersey didn't notice either. But two miles away, on the top of Pierce Hill, Maureen White looked out her bedroom window as she finished getting dressed and noticed.

"Hey, Ma," she yelled down the stairs. "There's smoke coming out of Daddy's house." She made her bed quickly, then she started in on her sister's bed, always a mess. Just like him, she thought; no, he's just like her, just like a twelve-year-old but worse. At least Jennifer knew the difference between right and wrong, even if she was a slob. But not her father. She tried not to think of him but she had already started and she couldn't just stop thinking, so she thought of him, and the hippie girl.

She never knew how the girl happened to be driving around on their back road. Even the mailman wouldn't drive that far back any more, now that Cecil's house was the only one there that had anybody in it. But outsiders always had a way of finding it, and this snazzy little car with Connecticut plates pulled up one June day when Maureen and her father were setting out the cabbage plants. Out came a girl with frizzy red hair wearing a long flowered skirt, her breasts bobbing up and down under a skimpy sleeveless shirt that would have made you think there wasn't a single blackfly in the whole of Maine.

"Jesus Christ," Cecil muttered. "What the hell do you think *she* wants?"

Maureen put down the watering can and watched as the girl sauntered towards them across the field. Cecil put down his box of plants and stared. They both stood there and stared as the girl came closer. Then Cecil growled at Maureen, "Well don't just stand there. Go fill up that can and get those rows ready."

The girl with Connecticut plates said she was wondering if there was a greenhouse around where she could get some cabbage plants. She had seen them planting and thought he looked like he might know.

Maureen was disgusted. They always thought he would know whatever it was they wanted just because he was too lazy to shave or get his hair cut more than once a year. They saw that mane of gray hair and the snarled beard and figured he was a hippie too. Stupid. And then he played along and talked nice and charming to them like he did to everyone else in the world who wasn't related to him. So what if he had a vocabulary bigger than all the rest of the people in town put together? He was smart, all right, but he could have done a lot better. All he did was read a bunch of junky catalogues and newspapers and shuffle around the Registry of Deeds all the time, trying to see if he could wheedle his way into some land he didn't own yet. But he never went past the eighth grade, and Maureen had already finished the tenth.

"So your friends bought the old Cobb place, you say?" He was pulling on his beard, remembering how many times the place had changed hands and who had paid what for it for the last fifty years. Same old story. Maureen went down to the creek.

"Oh yes, we got chickens, too," he was saying when she came back with the watering can full. "Only we also got a dog who eats eggs just as fast as they can lay 'em." The girl laughed and her breasts jiggled up and down.

Maureen watered the places where the cabbages would go and by the time she had gone up one row and come back down the next, the girl was skipping away toward her snazzy little car with a dozen cabbage plants in each hand.

She didn't find out until later that the girl had invited her father to have supper with her and her hippie friends up at the old Cobb place. Or that Cecil had gone and had supper with the whole crew of them and that the girl had taken her new fifty-four-year-old pet hippie into a canvas teepee and made love with him. And that the girl and her flowered skirt and frizzy hair and bobbing breasts had come back to see him the next day.

Once Maureen found out all this and what happened next, it had gotten stuck in her head like a record that ran in the same groove again and again until it made her stomach hurt. She couldn't get rid of it. As if she had been there all along, crouched in a corner somewhere, she saw how the hippie girl came back the next day when no one was there. She went back to the field and looked and yelled but Cecil wasn't there. She went towards the house, stepping over piles of horseshit all over the yard and picking her way around pieces of junk, old cars and tractors and rusty machinery that didn't work. She would not have had a chance to see the junk the day before. Maureen herself hadn't noticed it, really noticed it, for all those years. She fought with all her might to keep from seeing it, but now it was too late. Pulled every step of the way like a shadow, feeling almost as if she were as light and jaunty and cool and flowery as the girl herself, Maureen saw her life turned inside-out and upside-down through those smug hippie eyes, saw her home transformed in one blink into a nightmare.

The girl reached the house. She pushed her way past three sheep that wouldn't move and kicked at the pig that leaned against her knees trying to get through the doorway when she knocked. Sheep and pigs right at the door. Maureen winced every time she pictured it; why had it never bothered her before? Finally the girl pushed the door open as far as it would go — Maureen could feel the thud as it hit the edge of the table — and went in. There was so much crud on the windows she could hardly see, but she saw enough. Maureen saw it with her. Before it had been just the kitchen, just a regular mess. But now it was something worse, something awful. Something a girl could stick up her hippie nose at. There were mountains of dirty dishes, a rusty cookstove flooded with papers and beer cans and wilted cabbage plants, a lopsided table strewn with coffee-stained cups, ashtrays and beer cans and crumbs, a shredded linoleum floor littered with cigarette butts and pellets of animal feed, streamers of yellowed wallpaper curling off the walls, a crumbling ceiling soot-stained black, heaps of boots and clothes. Helplessly stuck in this groove in her head, Maureen watched the girl as she stumbled past the pig at the door, ran to the car and left.

Then she could picture the rest, somebody telling the girl all those rumors that even Maureen had heard before and knew were really just jokes and harmless. That ever since his wife walked out three years before, Cecil White would never bother to change his clothes until they rotted right off his back. Or that there were so many leaks in the roof that the tables and chairs would go floating around the house during a good spring rain, and if the door wasn't closed fast enough, the current would sweep them right outside. Suddenly all those rumors stopped being jokes when they were used to feed that uppity hippie scorn. Nothing felt the way it had felt before, once Maureen found it all out. All of it. How could that have happened to her, to have to learn it all? Cecil had gotten into one of his drunken fits and told everyone he could find that he'd gotten laid by the hippie girl. And the girl had not missed a chance, before she dismantled her teepee in a huff and went back to Connecticut, to tell what a pigsty she found at Cecil's. So that the whole uproarious joke of it was spilled to Maureen by a bunch of kids at Horace's store when she stopped with Aunt Ethel for a coke on the way to the lake. And then the record started getting stuck in her head.

She had wished she was dead, wished he was dead, wished they were all dead. To go running off with a hippie slut and be proud of it to boot! Here she'd been thinking no one was good enough for him and then this girl comes along and thinks she's *too* good for him. So much time she'd spent trying to make a home and going to school and doing the garden and keeping the animals from starving and never being able to keep up with it all, and then that hippie girl comes and does this to her. Too good for them! Letting everyone know how it was she lived, *really* lived, when even the poorest people around swept the floors and kept the pigs out of the kitchen and they weren't even all that poor. And she thought it had been worth it so she could ride the horses all day if she wanted or go to town with him when he let her or not eat breakfast or be ashamed. Somehow it had never felt wrong, before, to live the way they did, but now it was clearly wrong and everyone knew it was wrong and had always known and her father — oh how she could scream — her own father who had kept this such a secret from her gave it away now before she had a chance. Betrayal! To make such an unbelievable mess of it, going to bed with a stupid hippie. And the girl who was too good for them just upped and ran away and left her with the mess. How could she even go back to school?

"You run off with a slut and even a slut thinks you're a pig and you expect *me* to stay?" she had shrieked, hurling her clothes into a cardboard box.

"Slut, huh." He laughed and followed her to the car. "You think you're so good, just wait. You'll turn out to be a goddamned slut worse than that girl and it won't be my goddamned fault either."

Her mother started the car.

"Wait and see, you'll be back," he yelled.

She kicked hard against the car floor. "I never want to see you again as long as I live!"

And she hadn't seen him again in those two years.

"Ma, don't you hear me? I think Daddy's house is on fire!" Maureen's voice floated downstairs.

"No, silly," Eleanor said. "The smoke's from the chimney. Probably burning papers." She gazed out the window as she washed the dishes and spoke as if to the window itself.

"Hurry up, Mike, and finish your breakfast. Bring me your bowl, and Marian's too. Marian, finish putting your shoes on before you go out."

"Mommy, watcha gonna do about the smoke?" asked Jennifer, drying a bowl.

"Why Jenny, I just said, it's coming from the chimney. Your daddy and brother are burning some trash. Now try drying another bowl for a change so we can get this moving, okay? I've got to get to work."

"Suppose he burns up?" asked Wendy, the youngest.

Jimmy lumbered down the stairs shrieking in falsetto, "Mommy, Mommy, Daddy's on fire! Quick, get the marshmallows!"

The five kids fell into fits of nervous giggles, then howled freely and unmercifully until Maureen came down looking sullen and grabbed the rest of the bowls off the table.

"Hey, that's my Cheerios!" yelled Mike.

"Tough shit," she snapped.

"Watch your language," said Eleanor, stealing glances out the window. "See if you can't get this place vacuumed today, okay? And make sure Mike stays away from Horace's."

Maureen groaned. "They make such a *mess*."

Eleanor remembered the vacuum cleaner was clogged and

thought of the twenty-two years in that other house without a vacuum cleaner or a drop of running water or a bathroom or a furnace or a telephone. A telephone, ringing like hers was ringing right now. If he just had a phone like every other human being a person could call him up and find out if he was burning papers or lying there hung-over about to go up in flames in his own stinking bed.

It was Horace on the phone. "Hullo, Eleanor?" he began. "You see that smoke coming out of Cecil's place over there?"

"For as long as I've been living on your God-forsaken hill I can see everything you can see, Horace Pierce."

"Well, what d'ya make of it?"

"I'd say there's a fire in the stove."

"Eleanor, it's 75 degrees outside. It's gonna be hotter than hell all day long. You can't mean to tell me Cecil's lit a fire on a day like this, can you?"

"I can't mean to tell you anything about Cecil. Never could. It's none of my business now, thank the Lord."

"Well I think one of us ought to find out."

"You tell that man to put a phone in his house and then find out." She paused. "I don't know. Seems to me there's nothing strange about a little smoke. He's probably burning papers. Anyhow, Clayton's down there."

"You sure?"

"The boy lives down there, right?"

"Yup, when he's not out drunk."

"Listen, Horace. Cecil's lived in that shack with that stove for over fifty years and never burned himself up yet. But if it starts looking smokier by the time I leave for work, I'll call Wayne over to the firehouse."

"Then you'll take care of it."

"Yes, I'll take care of it. Now hurry along and get down to your store. You're late, you know, missing a lot of good business."

Horace would meddle. He'd round up everybody in town and get those fire trucks juiced up and go all the way down there just to watch Cecil burn his trash. And wouldn't Cecil love that.

There *did* seem to be just a little more smoke, though.

Making fools of people, that always was what he liked. Treating people like animals and animals like people. The only reason everybody liked him so much was because they didn't have to live with him and his filth. She always knew that if she hadn't been around to keep one step ahead of his trash-heap of a life he'd have become what he became, only sooner.

"You're such a slob, Cecil," she would say when he'd neglect to fix the roof or patch a window or scrape the muck off his shoes for the hundredth time.

"I'm a free man, Eleanor," he'd always answer.

"You're a slob and you married me and sweet-talked me into having eight children so you could make slobs out of us all."

"Would you rather make tea for the minister's wife?"

"You're no better than that pig out there, wallowing in your own filth."

"Would you rather wash and iron a different shirt for me every day of the week?"

"For five years you've fattened that pig. Every summer you say, 'This year we're going to eat that pig.' Every summer you fatten it up. And every winter you're afraid to slaughter it."

"Now who the hell gives a damn, besides you and the pig?"

"You're like some king of the barnyard, sitting on your throne of horse manure holding court and talking pretty to a bunch of useless animals."

"They're not useless; they're my friends."

"Friends! You buy horses and let them get scrawny and sell them at a loss. You lose money on every animal you own. Even your rabbits don't breed, Cecil."

"But you always said I was the smartest man around, remember? I was the original self-made man." He doubled over and cackled.

"Yes, and just look at you."

"So why the hell did you marry me?"

"Why? Because you tricked my father into selling you his prize mare and gave free rides on it to every kid in town. Because you bad-mouthed the President. Because I was a damned fool."

"You said at the time I had an open mind."

"Did I? Did I mention at the time that it was open at both sides and whatever garbage went in one end went right out the other and nothing passing through ever got you off your behind?"

"Ass."

"Ass, then."

"No, I don't seem to recall any such nonsense."

"Cecil, kill that pig."

Eleanor hadn't minded arguing with Cecil. It reminded her she was alive when she most needed to remember. There was something in his defiance, and, to a degree, in his filth, that appealed to her, drew her out of herself and her work and the unmitigated seriousness of it all. But he was so harsh and sarcastic. One minute he would be smart and clever, and the next minute he'd be downright mean. Well, the kids could take it. They were different from other kids and she liked them, and him, for that. They said what they meant and they'd grow up to be tough. Or maybe she was wrong; maybe they'd grow up to be drunks.

When things became really and deeply bad between them, she and Cecil did not rant and rave at each other. Like the January night five years before. She had been working the afternoon shift up at the shoe factory and when she got out that day there were six inches of snow on the ground and more falling in furious gusts. It took her an hour just to get to Ethel's to pick up Wendy and Marian. Then it took nearly another hour just to get to the crossroads. By the time she got home there were three-foot drifts in the driveway and it was nearly nine.

Cecil was sitting there in the living room drinking beer and reading a month-old newspaper. "Horace tow you up?" was all he said.

It was only when she had built up the fire and put something resembling dinner on to cook, found all the kids, fed the dogs, and started to clear the rubble off the table that she finally saw the telegram. It was already open. She was afraid to touch it, it could only be bad. And it was. Their oldest son had been killed in Vietnam.

It was still hard to remember how it went from there, to force herself to piece it together again. She had told the children, and they had wandered off to their own secret corners of the house, stunned and unbelieving; he had been gone so long anyhow, it had seemed, what the difference was now exactly, they weren't quite sure, she wasn't quite sure. And she had wept with the last bits of strength left in her, and pounded, and sat, and stared hard and long at nothing whatsoever, losing the thread of it all — his death, her grief, the meaning that was supposed to be there — in a hollow, echoing ball of numbness. She had lost control, and then she had picked it up, and lost it again, and she had wished the whole impossible truth would go away. Maybe a mistake had been made, maybe it was someone else — but no, it was somewhere in here that it had begun to sink in and make her head spin. And then the fog and ice and numbness had overtaken her in a painless, drunken sort of way and she sat for hours, wasn't it? It had seemed like days, even years, but probably it was not even hours. And after the dinner had long overcooked and the fire gone out too, and the stony silence sent chills through the rooms, she went back to Cecil, still drinking and reading.

"Why didn't you say anything?" she whispered.

He didn't look up from the paper. "Figured you'd find it soon enough. And you did."

"Cecil, Ross is dead," she said, still in whispers.

"Well, what did you expect to happen to him over there?"

"Cecil, you're talking about your son. Your *child!*"

And then he looked up at her, finally, with nothing in his face but drink and not even enough of that, and said, "There's plenty more where that one came from, you know."

She woke up then, as from a sharp slap across the cheek, and she knew that this could not be happening to her and if it was happening there was no excuse left for it. From somewhere the voice that was hers came through calm and flat. "Well then there's plenty of wives where this one came from too."

She and Wendy and Marian went back to Ethel's that night following close behind the state snowplow. Next day she got Mike and Jennifer and Jimmy. Clayton wanted to stay and she let him; he was old enough to know where he belonged. But Maureen wanted to stay, too.

"Leave?" she had gasped. "But I can't leave. The horses, Ma. I've got to stay with them. And how could I leave Daddy? He's the only one who talks to me in this family."

Maureen was bitter. Eleanor was bitter. She let Maureen stay.

Maybe she shouldn't have done it so fast. Maybe he had been upset, even cried before she got home. He had backward ways of showing emotion, always yelling at them when it was tenderness he must have meant, laughing at the kids when he should have been most proud, so gruff and heavy in his love-making. You never knew how a man like that might tackle his grief. But to be so disgustingly crude! No, he couldn't have cared. He never cared. It was possible, after all, that for twenty-two years those backward displays of emotion were just no emotion at all. She was right to leave; she would have had to have left soon enough anyway. He just did not care about a thing.

But he had never been so careless as to let his house burn down. And now the smoke was definitely thicker, less definitely coming from the chimney.

Now there was some sense to their lives. Breakfast was always at seven and dinner was always at six. There was a place for everything and everything was usually in its place. The lawn got mowed and the driveway got plowed. There was no rusty trash lying around, there were no dirty animals hovering by the door. The kids sometimes complained there was nothing to do anymore. Well, it wasn't as lively, that was true. But at least it was civilized. She could be a Mrs. Jones, say, from anywhere, instead of Mrs. Cecil White from right there. There could only be one Mrs. Cecil

White at any one time in the whole universe, and you could take it for just so long. It was better to be a Mrs. Jones and at least have running water and live in the twentieth century.

"Twentieth century be damned," she could hear him say.

"Cecil White be damned yourself," she mumbled out loud. Maureen spun around at the door and smiled. "Just what I was thinking," she said, and went out before Eleanor could say anything.

Now Maureen, she never would forgive him for that hippie girl. But if that hippie girl had had any sense, she would have stuck around and found just what she was looking for. She pretended to go back to nature, but when she got there she didn't like what she saw, no, not when it was Cecil. But if she'd just stayed and straightened it up a little — not to go cleaning out the closets or fussing around in the corners, but just polished it up so she could stand to look at it — they would have gotten along fine, two of nature's children. Foolish girl. No, Maureen could despise him for that if she wanted to, but not Eleanor.

Yet they were so much alike, she and Maureen. For the rest of their lives they'd both say it was his filth that drove them away, instead of his trampling on every decent human feeling like so much horse bedding. For the rest of their lives they would clean house with a vengeance trying to wipe out his indifference. Neither of them was ashamed to speak of his unspeakable squalor that they so willingly tolerated for all those years. Yet they never once mentioned, to each other or to anyone else, that the man who fed and clothed them, who amused them and gave their lives a focus, might very well not have given a damn about them. Might not have, or might have. How could they know? Was that the unutterable shame?

But then there was that pig. Four years after Eleanor left, when the pig was nearly ten years old, he finally slaughtered it, butchered it, and started in to eat on it. Tough as nails, they said, and didn't that story get around. Well, what did he expect? And then he sat on his doorstep and sobbed like a baby.

He still would not leave them alone. You could move to China and never get away from him. Here he was sending up smoke signals, only who could read them? "Save me, Eleanor," said the murky black clouds. But then the wisps curled around mocking, saying, "Let me play a good joke, let me have the last laugh."

The kids were upstairs, outside, gone. She had to go to work. She ran upstairs and got a sweater, came down, took her lunch out of the refrigerator, picked up her purse, and went out. Maureen was sitting on the front step. Eleanor stood next to her.

"Tomorrow they'll all be back in school and won't you be the happy one, huh, Maureen?"

"Look at that smoke, Ma."

"I see it."

"You can almost smell it from here."

"Nonsense."

"There's a lot more now, you know."

"Stop baiting me, Maureen."

"Well, why didn't you let Horace call? You should have let him do it."

That was it; she should have let Horace do it.

"I sure won't do it," Maureen taunted. "Don't expect *me* to call."

"Don't worry." Eleanor went over to the car and threw in her sweater and her purse and her lunch. She fidgeted with the keys, left the door open, and went back to Maureen, who snickered with annoyance.

"Why don't you go?"

Eleanor stayed, Maureen stayed, they stared into the valley watching the puffs of smoke.

"He could burn up in there, and then he'd keep on burning right through hell," said Maureen. "And you'd be stitching inner soles."

"And you?"

"Oh, I'll be drinking a coke and watching television and —"

"Shut up, Maureen," said Eleanor. She went into the house and picked up the phone.

CLAIRE'S SONG
a monologue in two acts   *Kendall Merriam*

for Claire Sikoryak

ACT I

The scene is a rather battered living room with indifferent furniture and decorations. The center stage is dominated by a large, obviously cheap green sofa in bad repair. On the sofa sits a small woman about forty-five with her hair up in curlers. She is wearing a faded bathrobe and slipper socks. She is trimming her nails with an emery board and chain-smoking cigarettes. A radio on the table beside the sofa is playing country songs.

She looks up and notices the audience —
she turns off the radio and speaks

There, that damned thing is off
I know it's not polite to listen
when you're trying to talk to someone
but I'm kinda addicted
But you see I do have some manners

I was brought up good and when
I think of it I have manners
my life hasn't been easy
so sometimes I forget'em
especially when I'm being hit around
by someone I don't like
Mind you I don't get hit too often
because I hit back
and that's known around town
so most of the men don't mess with me
excepting when they're drunk
then it don't hurt so much
I know I don't look like much
you probably think
I don't get asked out much
but I do
When I get these curlers off
and get into my glad rags
I look pretty good for a woman over forty
I'm not saying how much over
but it's not enough to worry about
I have one regular beau
Harry, Harry Blackman, Jr., that is
He's sweet to me and never hits me
but he's a bit too sweet
if you get my meaning
just not very exciting
even though he makes good money
and takes me places

Last winter, for example,
we went down to Orlando
I couldn't get enough of that Busch Gardens
and he took me to a different restaurant
every night — that's how sweet he is
but sometimes I like to get drunk
and he don't allow that
when I'm with him
he keeps saying
"Don't you think you've had enough,"
long before I've had enough
I may be a small woman
but I've always prided myself
on the way I can hold liquor
Once I had eight Black Russians
and kept on dancing
though that night I was pretty sick
when I got home
The house reeled for two days
after that
I haven't had a Black Russian since
but nothing else holds me back
right now I'm into Margaritas
I change every couple of months
Met one guy in a bar last week
said he would invent a drink for me
called it a Golden Russian
vodka, banana liqueur and a cherry
Ugh, it was awful

and the cherry was way out of date
if you get my meaning
The next night I was in the same bar
and he was inventing the same drink
for another lady
that's probably the oldest new drink
in creation
But I don't want you to think
that I work the bars as a profession
I just like the scene
No, I work in the sardine factory
over to Wiscasset
and since I'm the second fastest packer
they've got
they employ me almost full time
even when there's no fish
Sometimes we pack frog legs
shipped in from India of all places
the labels have all this fancy French writing
but they come from India
I can imagine the price put on them
They smell so bad
I'd never eat one, I can tell you
but then I never eat Maine sardines either
if I can't get Norwegian
I don't eat 'em at all
though once I had some Polish ones
that were pretty good
probably caught off here anyway

But why am I telling you this boring shit
you didn't come here to
hear about a sardine factory
you probably would rather
hear about my love life
but I'm not sure I'm going to tell you
We may get to it later on
but you'll have to pay extra
for the good stuff
Ha! Ha! Ha!
that's a laugh
you think I'm just a seedy tramp
I'm sure
but I was born to royalty
even if I don't look it now
My parents' name was Behuzov
just like Pierre
in *War and Peace*
but when my parents came here
just before World War Two
they changed to Bellows
because my father was a blacksmith
and that was the first
English word he learned
You may ask what royalty was doing as
a blacksmith
well the family fortune
was wiped out by the Bolshies
and father had to learn to shoe horses

He was a great strong man
and could do it easy
so it was natural to him
but my parents, both dead now, bless 'em
told me and showed me papers
that showed we had had an estate
in White Russia
before the Revolution
I was born in Germany
and we got out just in time
and my father
worked at the Iron Works
during the war
He always got the award for best worker
he was damned anxious to put those Germans under
he hated their guts
for the way they had treated him
There's a word in German that means
what they did to my father
untermen, something like that
I can't remember
but it made him hate them with a passion
and he made me promise
I would never have a German boyfriend
which I never have
except for once, one night
that was with a guy named Klaus,
a photographer
over here for some German magazine

I met him in a bar
one night
about ten years ago
and we hit it off
I told him what my father said
and he said that was silly
he was only a child during the war
and wasn't to blame
Anyway that night was good
one of the best
on the top floor of the Hotel Sedgewick
just a year before it burned
I remember the pink of the curtains
just matched the tip of you know what
But he had to leave for New York the next day
and I never heard from him again
except once I got a postcard
that came to the factory from him
from somewhere in South America
I wonder what he was doing down there
it sure would be nice if he came back
one night more of that
kind of loving wouldn't hurt
So I think my Daddy was wrong
good loving has no nationality
but I've never been with a Russian
so I don't know how they are
but one of my friends
showed me an article in *Penthouse*

that said they weren't very good
I'd like to try for myself sometime
but I don't suppose I'll get the chance
the way things are between the Russkies,
my home town
and the good old U.S. of A.
No, I think the best I ever had
was a French Canadian from Montreal
I met down to Old Orchard
he drew it out
like none of my American friends could
I go back there every summer
but have never hit it lucky again
When you think of all the times
I've done it
only about five stand out in my mind
and they were always
one-night stands
Oh, well, maybe I'll meet someone tonight
this being Saturday
and a holiday at that
I'll have to remember
not to get shit-faced
so I can enjoy it if it comes to me
Let's change the subject
this is making me too sad
thinking of all I've missed
and me getting along to the time
when I'll dry up

I've asked some of the older women
at the plant what it's like after
and they say it's still good
but not as good
so I better get my licks in now
Jesus, how time flies
I wonder if I would have been better off
if there hadn't been any Revolution
and I'd been royalty
like my father said we was
You may not believe this
but I've read *War and Peace*
four times — once all the way through
and three other times the love parts
they weren't much happier than I am
I think with all the wars and deaths
I tried to read *Dr. Zhivago*
but couldn't get into it
But I've seen the movie six times
I always imagine myself
in the role of Julie Christie
I just can't wait for the scene
where she and Omar Sharif meet in the library
that has to be the top scene
That's why I go to the library
every week
I don't like to read that much
but I'm always thinking
that I'm going to meet Omar Sharif sometime

I don't read most of the books
I take out
but I keep going
I actually did get a date there once
— an Irishman who was there on St. Patrick's Day
he took me dancing
in Portland that night
and it was the best dancing I ever had
but he got so drunk he couldn't do anything
if you get my meaning
But I keep going to the library anyway
every Saturday afternoon
unless there is fish
or I'm too lazy like today
Anyway I've got something lined up for tonight
so I don't have to go looking
This is a new guy so I even bought
a new dress at Senter's
I should look pretty good
I may be small
but I can look pretty good
if I like the guy
and I put my attention to it
I've got to go out and do something
happy tonight
I'm all torn up inside
yesterday would have been my son's
eighteenth birthday
if he had lived

He was killed in a crash
when he was ten years old
back in '74
his father had taken
him to a baseball game at Fenway Park
and got drunker than a skunk
and crashed into the tollbooth
on the New Hampshire Turnpike comin' home
He, my ex, Frank Johnson
wasn't hurt a bit
but Teddy was thrown out through
the window of the pickup
and was killed instantly
Thank God for that
at least he didn't have to suffer
I beat up Frank something furious
when he got back
and I wouldn't let him come
to the funeral
— stupid bastard —
He had promised me he wouldn't drink
but I should've known better
Teddy was my only baby
and I had to have my tubes tied
after he was born
so there wasn't a chance for anyone else
Teddy Kennedy Johnson
I named him after Teddy Kennedy
as you can guess

it happened a funny way
I was living in Beverly, Mass.
when I was pregnant
and was shopping downstreet
just when they was opening
Kennedy's campaign headquarters
and he was there
that good-looking Irishman
so I went over to him
and said, "You can't kiss my baby
but you sure can kiss me."
and he did
and when he did he said
"Name it after me."
so I did
Teddy was very proud of his name
and had started a scrapbook
about Teddy Kennedy
My Teddy was real bright
and might have made a good politician
at least he would have gone to college
and got out of this rat race I'm in
(holds face in hands and sobs a little)
There, that's over
I didn't mean to tell you this
but it just comes out
even though it happened
eight years ago
It's like it was yesterday

I had so many hopes for Teddy
now there's nothing
I'm thinking of sponsoring
one of those orphans
that you see in the magazines
maybe I'll send one of them to college
I've got four thousand saved up for it already
I guess I never accepted that he was dead
They didn't let me see him
closed casket and all
Sometimes I think it is a big joke
someone pulled on me
and he is going to walk into the room
but I know better
Well, let's get off that subject
you didn't come here to be sad
you came for entertainment
and the only two things
that I know are entertaining
are music and sex
and since I can't sing a note
it'll have to be the other
The man who is taking me out tonight
looks pretty good
but I don't know how
he will perform
a real sharp dresser
but about thirty pounds overweight
he's a shoe salesman

over to Cook's Corner
and hasn't been out for a year
since his divorce
he's ten years younger than me
but he doesn't know that
and I'm his first woman
in over a year
so he should be anxious to please
I don't think he's a drinker
but you never can tell
if he is I'll ditch him
We're going over to the Sheraton
to dine and dance
and there's always a couple of the boys
that I know from Bath
who'll give me a ride home
if you get my meaning
I know I must sound like a slut
but I ain't
I only fooled around once
when I was married
and that wasn't serious
But after I got divorced
I had to keep in circulation
and after Teddy died
I felt that I didn't have anything to lose
reputation or nothing
So I played while that cat was away
I don't care nothing about food

you can see I'm thin
and I don't really care
about clothes except they get me around
and I earn good money because
I'm on piecework
most of the time
sometimes I can make $300 a week
and you can see I don't spend it
on this dump
so I have plenty to do with
Like I said I've got $4,000
in the bank
and if I don't give that to some orphan
I'll take a trip
to Jamaica
or some place on an island
and blow it all
just about the only thing
I blow it on is my car
Two years ago
I bought a white Volvo P-1800
completely restored
up at Reilly's Imports
$8500 cash I paid
they were kinda snooty
so I told them I was a doctor's wife
That thing goes like a bat
just like the Saint
drove it on TV

that's where I got the idea, of course
I've had lots of offers for it
but I'll never sell
one guy offered me $12,000
because they're so hard to get
in good condition
but I'll never sell
I love to pull up in the plant parking lot
and see the other women
getting out of their
Chevies and Toyotas
don't they envy me!
they know I got style
Sometimes the car gets me in trouble
I never drive it when I'm drunk
but sometimes men who drive Porsches
come around if they see me parked somewhere
I'm not up to that crowd socially, you see
personally I like the men
who drive the Chevies and Toyotas
but sometimes a real smooth talker
comes over and starts a conversation
about the car
Usually I know enough to get out of there
but once this guy come up to me
and asked me to go to his apartment with him
it had steel floors and black leather walls
and I was very afraid
He had me tie him up and hit him with a whip

he kept yelling "Harder! Harder!"
but I couldn't
so I got out of there
left him tied up
I never saw his name in the paper
so I guess someone let him out
Jesus, that scared the piss out of me
so I never talk to anyone about my car
I just drive it
Sometimes I get on 95
and drive like hell up to Bangor
and eat at Dysarts truck stop
and talk to the truckers
if you get my meaning
but I never take it out of state
I'm afraid it will have an accident
or get ripped off
so I just drive it here in Maine
where it's safe
my pride and joy
I call it "Marion"
after an old aunt I had
She wasn't really an aunt
just an old lady in the neighborhood
in Bath where I grew up
but she gave me cookies and lemonade
and told me stories
something I missed since all my folks
were back in Russia

Yep, Marion is quite a car
once I raced a policeman
up 95 and beat him
didn't get arrested either
I asked him if I could do it
and he agreed
that was one of the most fun times
I've ever had
Well, I don't have to worry about Marion tonight
Jack is going to pick me up
and we're going in his old Ford
it won't be style
but I guess it'll get us there
The food at the Sheraton sucks
or at least it did last time I was there
but they have a country band
which, as you already know, is my kind of music
and if Jack isn't a good dancer
my friend Clyde will be there to fill in
He's a fifty-eight-year-old black guy
with eleven kids
but can he dance
and yes I do know where them kids came from
if you get my meaning
I have no prejudices
any man who treats me right
I treat right
and except for the guy with the Porsche
and a few drunks

I've left'em all satisfied
I've got a good reputation
around the Bath-Brunswick area
as an interesting woman
so I have plenty of dates
Some of you out there
might not think it's much of a life
I know you're looking down on me
"sardine-packing slut"
you're saying
but that ain't right
I've made my way
and not depended on my royalty
for anything
I've read a couple of books besides
War and Peace
and I know what it was like
and what it is like there
so I think I'm doing pretty good
and if I want to have a little fun
so what?
The Good Book says we only last seventy years
so I'm going to get the most out of it
even if it hurts
which it does sometimes
but then everybody has their troubles
and I'm still alive
Why Stella, my best friend at the plant
just found out she had lung cancer

which is why I've got to give up
these damned things
(*stubs out a cigarette*)
I have a pretty easy life all told,
if you consider sardine canning easy
it seems to come natural to me
I've never, ever cut myself
not even on the first day
when I was only sixteen
I like everybody at work
except Dinky Small
one of the supervisors
His real name is Daniel
and he doesn't allow anybody
to call him Dinky
but I do
because he torments me about being Russian
by calling me "Red"
or he'll say
"How's the little Communist today"
I always say
"I'm true blue American, Dinky"
and he doesn't like that
for Christ's sake I was naturalized
when I was eleven
I bet I know more than he does
about American history!
I once asked him
who Lincoln's first Vice President was

and he didn't know
even though it was Hannibal Hamlin
who was from Bangor, Maine
Imagine that!
But the bastard never lets up on me
he calls me a Communist
at least twice a day
he claims he was in the army in the Korean War
but someone once told me
he spent most of it in the brig
in Japan for hitting an officer
For one thing he's jealous of me
because he makes less money
because supers don't get piecework
and he's got a bunch of kids
to feed
his wife works at the plant sometimes
and she is the most dragged-out woman
I know
I feel sorry for the poor thing
If that bastard was to ever put a hand
on me
I'd cut him right in the guts
with my scissors
with all the fish guts on them
He'd get an infection
he'd never forget
One of my buddies at the plant
said he told her that he wanted to fuck me

and I told her to tell him
that he'd have to wait till I was dead
before I'd let him near me
so he knows
But he keeps picking at me
I don't let it bother me too much
I guess you can't always have a good thing
it's the only thing I don't like about work
the rest is easy
I let Gail Coffin
be number one girl
so I don't have to go to the contest
at the Lobster Festival
over to Rockland
and I rake in the same amount of money
as she does
and I have a free life
No one else there
drives a car like Marion
and nobody has as many boyfriends
as I do
Of course most of 'em got kids
so I am at a disadvantage there
but I enjoy life more
at least I think so
The others are always
coming up to borrow money
or beg a ride at noontime
because they've never been in a car

that can go like Marion
No it's a pretty good life
and I can't complain too much
if my parents had stayed in Germany
I'd probably be dead
or married to some kraut
but instead I'm in the land of the free
and can go out with a different man
every night of the week
if I choose
or I can call up Harry
and he'll take me to New York
or Florida
the only thing is
that he thinks someday
when I settle down a little
I'll marry him
But I've told him time and again
that I ain't gonna marry anybody
no matter how much they got in the bank
or between their legs
if you get my meaning
No, my life is pretty good
now, if I could only convince
myself of that
I'd probably be happy
But have you ever seen anyone who's happy
really happy?
I'll bet you ten-to-one

that they're lying through their teeth
nobody's happy
Why is it all the women at work
think they'd be happy
if they had their first boyfriend back
and not the one they're going with now?
I *married* my first boyfriend
and after the first year
I wasn't happy
Frank was pretty good in bed
he was a fair wage earner
he was good-looking
a good dresser
but he was a beginning drunk
and I didn't see that
when I married him
and it brought
the worst time of my life
Jesus, it was hard enough
for me to have a kid in the first place
It took three years of trying
and then the Doctor said no more
I had to have a Caesarean
because I'm so small
and they said I couldn't have any more
and then that bastard
goes and kills the
only child I had
Sometimes when I think of it

I think about buying a gun
and going to New Hampshire
where he lives now
and blowing his balls off
He's remarried
he was only in prison two years
"negligent homicide with a motor vehicle"
they called it
and gave him only two years
now he's got two kids
and what have I got — nothing
he's even got his license back
and drives a big Torino
Oh! I keep tabs on him
just in case
He don't know it
but I hired a detective
to find him after he got out of prison
and he does a sixth month check
just to let me know where he is
It costs me a few bucks
but I consider that money well spent
Sometime I may surprise myself
and do something about him
bastards like him don't deserve
to live
He never had a scratch on him
from the accident
but he had plenty

after I got through with him
I think now I should have done a complete job
I'd be out of prison by now
and that bastard wouldn't have the chance
to do any more harm
The detective says
Frank doesn't drink any
that he can find out
and goes to AA regular
but if I know him
that is just for show
I'm sure
Well, I'd better get off this subject
it's time to think about
getting these curlers out
Jack will be here in an hour or so
and I'm getting a little hungry
Even though I told you I don't like to eat
I am partial to shrimp cocktail
and sometimes they have good ones
at the Sheraton
sometimes I order three shrimp cocktails
and have nothing else
except my drinks
Some men consider me an expensive date
because of it and they complain a little
but if this Jack isn't feeding me a line
and really hasn't been out for a year
he should be willing to pay

and I'll pay him back
if you get my meaning
So if you folks will excuse me
I've got to take a piss
pardon the language
and I'll be back
after I take my shower
if the damned thing has any hot water
and we'll talk over
a few things on my mind
till Jack comes
so long for a bit.

(End of Act I)

ACT II

Scene: The couch is removed and center stage is a white dressing table with a rectangular mirror frame attached above it. A coat rack stands beside it. The table is covered with various perfumes and cosmetics. The actress comes out carrying her dress and shoes — she is wearing a white slip — she hangs her dress on the rack and puts her shoes on the floor. During this act she is putting on makeup and fixing her hair in whatever her normal sequence is.

There, all clean,
thank God there was some hot water
almost a miracle around here
I'll make myself real pretty
for Jack
so he gets his money's worth
I always try to please
I just wish more of them
would try to please me
life wouldn't be quite so bitter then
Oh! I know I've had a good life
except for Teddy dying
so I really shouldn't complain
I just get so lonely sometimes
Do you ever get lonely?
Do you think you have passed
through life like a shooting star?
I do sometimes
I think that I'm just a flash in the pan

and that life is so short
that we hardly exist at all
I want to *mean* something
not just for a night
but for a long time
But I can't see my way clear
to do what it takes
I mean I'm fairly intelligent
and a hard worker
but I know that my obit
will only be a couple of lines
in the *Times-Record*
Is that what it's all about?
I think of that movie "Alfie"
starring that gorgeous hunk
Michael Caine
you know the Englishman
I always think over that line
from the theme song
"What's it all about, Alfie?"
in a way I'm like Alfie
I go from man to man
and can't settle down
and make something of my life
Of course I know most of you
will continue to influence things
because you have kids
but I can't do that
(*holds face in hands for a minute*)

No! I see the end of my life
in some dark, dank nursing home
with nobody to look after me
I guess that's why I live life so hard now
I don't want to get old
but I can see it coming
right here in this mirror
there, got that wrinkle
(applies powder around corner of mouth)
but some day I won't be able to
I've seen some women
grow old gracefully
but I know I won't
I've got to grab on to something
I'll probably get married again
if Mr. Right comes along
but most of the men I know now
are boozers
and I'll never marry another boozer
even if I have to go to an unmarked grave
I have a little life insurance policy
for a couple of thousand
just to pay for my stone
right there in the cemetery
beside Teddy
I feel like being buried in Marion
so I can ride the highways of heaven or hell
whichever place I end up at
but I suppose the Cemetery Committee

wouldn't allow that
I don't know why I'm
sounding like *True Confessions*
I don't often get to talk to
a captive audience like you
most of the men I go out with
like to talk about sports and sex
and it never gets serious
but I'm a woman with a big heart
and want to discuss
things that mean a lot
I keep thinking this next guy
will be different
Why I've even been out
with two Bowdoin professors
and they're no better than the rest
just want to get into bed with me
seeking out the lowlife
of the town
which I guess means me
Sometimes I join those
pen-pal clubs but all they want
is to come over here from Korea
or someplace
I mean that's why I listen
to country music
all those sad songs
about cheating
and losing love

I feel sometimes that they were meant
for me and me alone
Once I even took a course
at UMP
Psychology I it was called
I thought I would try to understand myself
but it was all so confusing
especially when I met the professor
in a bar after class
and he tried to make me
just like everybody else
that was the extent
of my college career
I would try church if I thought it would help
but it doesn't
I couldn't get used to those
barroom faces from Saturday night
all decked out and pious
on Sunday morning
No, church ain't the answer
and there doesn't seem to be anything else
and I can't always be working
or driving Marion
When I get alone with myself
I'm a pretty desperate woman
and I don't know how to change that
Oh, well! you didn't come
to hear me bitch and moan
you want some entertainment

How about a joke?
One day Ralph and DooDah
were out in the woods
cutting pulp logs
when a tree fell on DooDah
after the police arrived
they said that Ralph
would have to go and tell DooDah's wife
But he didn't know exactly how to give her the bad news
so he went and knocked on the door
when DooDah's wife came to the door
Ralph sang this little song
"Somebody died in the woods today
DooDah, DooDah!"
Ha Ha Ha! Don't you think that's funny?
It was told to me by Frenchy Pilette
who told it with an accent
that made it even funnier
I laughed for half an hour after I heard that
(*Starts crying*)
Jesus, Jesus, Jesus
when is something good
going to happen in my life
I need something to drink
(*goes offstage and comes back
with an opened bottle of beer*)
There, maybe this will cheer me up
get a head start on tonight
(*takes a long swallow*)

Ugh! That tastes flat
it sure ain't the beer
that made Milwaukee famous
I wonder how long it will be
before I can't stand my looks
and have to have a fact lift?
I've already checked out a good clinic
in Boston
and know when the time comes
I'll be able to pay for it
As I said before
I won't grow old gracefully
the fur will fly when
they try to take me to
a nursing home
No, I intend to dance
right to the end
For my funeral
I don't want no organ music
I'd rather have Doug Kershaw
playing some lively Cajun tunes
on the fiddle
go out in style, I will
Here, I better get this makeup on
because Jack will be here
any minute
(puts on eye-shadow)
I wonder who'll
be at the Sheraton tonight

maybe some new guys
to dance with
I think Jack is too much of a porker
to be light on his feet
so I might have to provide
for myself
if you get my meaning
At least they have Dick Curless singing
there tonight
so there should be quite a crowd
Jack said he'd made reservations
so we should be able to get in
after I have my shrimp
In spite of my everlasting sadness
I know how to have a good time
so I'll just leave all my
bad thoughts
here with you
and enjoy myself
I'll have to remember
not to drink myself silly
I need to keep getting those
discounts on shoes
Jack gives me
Makes me feel good to get a bargain
based on my looks
I don't look forty-five do I?
There, it slipped out
and I promised not to tell you

you won't tell Jack will you?
He's only thirty-five
and I don't think
that an older woman
would appeal to him
I told him I was thirty-six
and he believes it
I am pretty well preserved
don't you think?
It must be all that fish oil
Ha! Ha! Ha!
it's a wonder
sometimes I have to take
two showers a day
to get rid of the smell
and washing my clothes is a horror
but I always change before
I get in Marion
it wouldn't do to have her smelling
like sardines in mustard pack
(puts on lipstick)
No! the old plant
smells something fierce
they've been using it
almost ninety years
and many a dead fish
has gone to some man's belly
from the place
Some people think I should be too ashamed

to work there
but it's honest work
and except for Dinky
it beats office work any day
and pays better
How many secretaries
do you see driving
a P-1800?
Yes, I sound so confident
when I'm talking about Marion
but sometimes I don't feel that way
I guess that's why
my friendships with men
are so whacked out
It goes back to my childhood
I was raped by a friend of my father's
when I was thirteen
but I didn't know it was rape
This friend, Bob,
sometimes watched us kids
when Mother and Dad went out
on Saturday nights
He always wanted to wrestle
with us two girls
and he let his hands
wander pretty freely
One time — it was real cold —
the folks got stuck at a party
in West Bath

and couldn't get the car started
so Bob had to watch us all night
I remember he had on his longjohns
he came into my room about one o'clock
in the morning
and this thing was sticking out
of his underwear
he made me touch it
and took off all my clothes
and put it in me
it hurt pretty bad
but I didn't dare fight him
he was so big
he made me swear I wouldn't tell my parents
but I did after two weeks
of not eating hardly any food
Mother kept asking what was wrong
and finally I told her
My father went to Bob
and beat the shit out of him
and made him leave the state
but the damage was done
and I couldn't look anyone in the face
for over a year
I was a senior in high school
before I would date anyone
and then I was real careful
I would only go out with the religious boys
so I wouldn't be found out

by boys who were fast
Frank was the first man I went with
and I waited to do it
until we were almost married
So that's why today
anyone who goes out with me
has to pay and pay
I never will get over
what the first man did to me
and because of that
I don't really enjoy sex that much
except when I know it's going
to be only for one night
and I will never see him again
You may think I'm stupid to feel this way
but I can't help it
Once I read somewhere
that one-fourth of the women
in America are molested
by the time they're eighteen
I've never talked about this before
but chances are that right in
this audience there are quite a few women
who have gone through
something like I have
and are still regretting it
I know this isn't a pretty story
but you came here to find out the truth
about me

and since you paid the piper
I will tell you the truth
That's one of the reasons
I have been so lonely
all my life
I never could confess to anyone
what was done to me
so forgive me if I seem promiscuous
I'm just getting
a little revenge
(takes a sip of beer)
No, my life has been pretty awful
in some ways
and I don't think my mother
ever forgave me
she seemed to think
that I had encouraged
this Bob character
but I didn't
Dad knew I was right
but Mother
when she got real mad at me
for not cleaning up my room
or helping with the dishes
would sometimes call me
a little hussy
and once she even accused me
of setting Bob up
because I think she liked him

more than my father knew
and once a year or so before
it happened
I caught them kissing
in the bathroom
So she blamed me
for rushing Bob out of her life
I think she thought
I was competing with her
for his attention
but I swear that was
the furthest from my mind
I always thought
he was sort of an uncle
who liked to play games with us
when he babysat
so there you have the big event
I should say
the black event
of my life
and whenever I see any man
who looks even vaguely
like Bob
I shudder
in spite of the fact that
it has been thirty-two years
since it happened
Oh! I like men well enough now
and most of them are gentle with me

but I always carry
a sharpened nail file with me
just in case
Thank God I never have had to use it
but I'm always on the look out
that's another reason
I don't like boozers
sometimes they act too strong
and I get nervous
about what will happen
but I'm pretty good about
defending myself
But sometimes when I'm with a guy
and we've done it
I wake up in the middle of the night
in a cold sweat
and get out of bed
and dress and call a taxi
and get the hell out of there
the men don't know what
to make of it
and I've lost some good friends
that way
but I can't help it
I think you can see why
From the time it happened
until I was twenty
I got very religious
ordinarily we only went to church

once a year
up to the little Russian church
in Richmond
on Russian Easter
but my parents were too lazy
to go the rest of the year
and I needed a closer God
so my friend Marie
invited me to go to the CYO
in Bath
and I went to church all the time
with her
though I was never confirmed
or anything
but the priests didn't know that
and I used to go to confession
every week
after Marie had told me
what to say
Yes, I confessed all my little
childhood sins
that didn't amount to a hill of beans
but I never could
as much as I tried
confess about the rape
it seemed too dirty
to bring into the church
so I went around with this big burden
and because of it I didn't do well in school

Once the guidance counselor
gave me a special test
and he said I could do college work
if I wanted to
but I didn't want to
and that's why
I'm in the fish factory today
life has been kind of a waste
and I wonder sometimes why I keep going
I ask Marion that
every time I drive up to Bangor
It would be so easy to
cross the lane
into a pulp truck
and nobody would ever know the difference
but I made up my mind that
I wasn't good enough
to commit suicide and
that I would have to suffer
life out
no matter what
Now that you've heard all that
you probably think
I'm a pretty sad person
and you'd be almost right
but sometimes I have fun
in spite of myself
Here I'll show you
I'll tell another joke

this was one my father
told about once a week
In the thirties
Russia tried to get
the people who had emigrated
after the Revolution
to come back
it offered a kind of amnesty
so one guy from Boston
decided that he would try it
now he knew from the start
that he wouldn't be able
to write back to his family
how conditions were
so he said that he
would send back a picture
of himself with a group of relatives
and if he was standing up
that meant things were ok
but if he was sitting down
things weren't so good
After six months
the picture came back
and he was lying down!
Ha! Ha! Ha!
(starts crying again)
that's so funny
it makes me cry
I miss my Daddy

just to think
I could have been royalty
if the world hadn't
turned upside down
now I'm only princess of the sardine factory
a big comedown
but at least I earn my own way
and I'm beholden
to nobody
Once I was in the nut ward at Regional
and some guy there
kept giving me little
presents
that didn't cost very much
candy bars and books
and once because I wasn't eating
a poem about funny
kinds of food
I was so depressed
I couldn't react
and one time
he sat beside me
and touched my hand
and I pulled it away
and got up
and left the room
It might have been my chance
to find somebody good
and I threw it away

anybody who could like me
in such a state
has to see qualities in me
that I can't see myself
but this is not the place for regrets
we're all entitled to a mistake or two
but I wonder if I'll ever
find someone
who loves me for myself
not for my bodywork
or my car
The men at the Sheraton
like to dance with me
and I'm sure would
fuck me too
but that's not what I mean
I need to have some tender loving
with the emphasis on tender
but I've never had it
not even Frank
did that for me
though I mistook it for the real stuff
the first year or so
No it's probably my fate
to go through life
without any satisfaction
but I can't help
wondering what sin I committed
to make God so angry at me

Sometimes I wonder if anybody
is happy
I wonder if all your faces
looking up at me
if any of you at heart
are really happy
if you were you probably
wouldn't be here
No, you came to listen
to someone else's troubles
to assure yourself
that you're better off than me
but maybe you're not
or you would be alone tonight
with a real true love
if such a thing exists
I know it's getting late
and you're already thinking
of what drink
you're going to order
at the Dolphin
but listen to me carefully
You're on the merry-go-round
and the brass ring
may be coming around your way
so grab it if you can
don't be like me
and let it go
it's never come around for me

that I can remember
but I'm still hoping
that's probably
why I'm singing for you now
I'm hoping that this Jack
who's going to pick me up
will be it
though I know in my heart of hearts
he ain't it
but some of you might still have a chance
(takes the last of the curlers out
and shakes her head to fluff up her curls)
That's him at the door now
I'll just let him wait a minute
so he won't be sure of himself
(puts on dress and shoes)
So long now
I hope you remember some
of what I've said
you may be the lucky one
(Exits)

(End)

INSIDE VACATIONLAND New Fiction from the Real Maine

DESIGN & COVER ILLUSTRATION by Sheila Garrett, South Harpswell, Maine

TYPOGRAPHY by Type & Design, Brunswick, Maine

PRINTED on acid-free paper and smyth-sewn by Maple-Vail Book Manufacturing Group, York, Pennsylvania

OTHER BOOKS from the Dog Ear Press include
A LIFE IN COMMON, poems by Mitchell Goodman
HERE COMES EVERYBODY'S DON'T BOOK, visual satire by Bern Porter
THE BOOK OF DO's, visual satire by Bern Porter
NOT FAR FROM THE MOUNTAINS OF THE MOON, fiction by Kala Ladenheim
HEART IN UTTER CONFUSION, takes on the erotic poetry of India, by Steve Kowit
SLEEPING IN AFRICA, poems by Dawn McGuire
DAUGHTERS WITHOUT MOTHERS, poem/testimony by lee sharkey
POETS ON PHOTOGRAPHY, edited by Mark Melnicove

For a complete list and catalogue write: The Dog Ear Press
P.O. Box 143
South Harpswell, Maine 04079